ERIMEM

ANGEL OF MERCY

Julianne Todd, Claire Bartlett

& Iain McLaughlin

THEBES PUBLISHING

ERIMEM

ANGEL OF MERCY

CONTENTS

ANGEL OF MERCY

1

Julianne Todd, Claire Bartlett and Iain McLaughlin

PART ONE

NO FUTURE

Julianne Todd, Claire Bartlett and Iain McLaughlin

An interesting by-product of having access to a machine that can send you absolutely anywhere in time and space is that TV loses its appeal. *X-Factor*. *Britain's Got Talent*, *The Voice…* why bother with them if I can go to a time machine and send myself back to see Elvis Presley in 1956 or Frank Sinatra in the forties? Hell, I can go back and see Mozart or Beethoven if I want to. I am definitely – definitely for one hundred percent totally sure and certain – going back to see the Beatles play in the Cavern in '61 or '62.

I've always been a fan of science fiction. Quietly. I didn't tell people about it much when I was a kid. Who wants to wear the tag of 'geek' or 'nerd' or 'saddo'. By the time I realised that anybody who would a) think liking science fiction was enough reason to insult somebody and b) actually insult somebody with any of those terms wasn't actually worth knowing, life had caught up and I'd lost interest in being one of the cool kids. Us Geeks have our own kind of cool. Smart-cool. Geek-chic.

I'd caught a bit of classic Star Trek on YouTube (the remastered ones with the gorgeous new special effects) while I was waiting for Matt to get ready to go out. He was spending the night at a friend of his. It was a friend I knew, nice family, and the friend's mum was always a good laugh so I was okay with it.

I was also just not in the mood for another of his "You're not Mum, Andy. You're only my sister!" rants. I know he's a teenager, I know he's been through a lot and I know it's not easy for him dealing with how life is now.

But does he have to be such a dick?

I think he's started looking at stuff he shouldn't online. I don't want to spy on his browsing habits but the autofill in Firefox on the laptop has been telling tales on him. Blondes with pneumatic knockers, most of them. Never understood those huge breast enlargements myself. They just look *sore*. I'd be scared they burst when I rolled over in bed. God knows, I wear a D cup and I have trouble enough with them. Those blondes must be up at GG or FF – which I assume stands Good God or For Fuc… let's not go there. Still, I do need to talk to Matt about that.

Really looking forward to *that*.

Almost as much as telling him about my taste in women. He's not ready for that conversation.

Neither am I.

I cycled across to Ibrahim and Helena's flat at about ten in the morning. It was one of those brilliant Saturdays when I wasn't working in the café. The students would have to bug somebody else for their bacon rolls… but never at ten in the morning on a Saturday. No chance. Half of them wouldn't have made it to bed yet.

Well, not their own beds anyway.

I'm never quite sure what time Erimem will surface from her bed. 'Whenever she feels like it' would seem to be the answer. Helena says Erimem is a nightmare to get moving for Uni some mornings. Other days she's bouncing about like Bambi on acid.

'Good practice for when we have kids,' I saw Helena tell Ibrahim once.

He almost choked on his coffee.

Helena's always taking the piss out of him. But they should have kids. They'd be great parents.

This was one of the days when Erimem was up early. By the time I arrived she had already been swimming in the Nile (okay, the replica of the Nile I programmed into the grounds of her Habitat. After that she'd been to the shop and had managed to buy milk and fruit – using real cash money which she is getting the hang of – and she'd done it without falling out with anybody. Moving to another country would be difficult enough for anybody. She's moved to a different country and a different time where there's almost nothing recognisable from her own.

It's no wonder she seems a bit dour and grumpy sometimes. Truth is she's got a wicked sense of humour when she relaxes.

She was in the kitchen with Helena when I arrived. Ibrahim was on his way out for a run. I told him it was starting to rain. He ran back indoors.

'Didn't really fancy a run this morning anyway,' he said, shutting the door behind us.

In the kitchen Helena pointed at a chair and told me to sit down. Erimem offered me some fruit. I said no, but then started picking at bits of fruit from her bowl. She just looked at me with a raised eyebrow then shoved the bowl between us so we could both pick at it.

'What are you planning to do today?' I asked Erimem.

She popped a strawberry into her mouth and smiled. I knew what the smile meant. She was going to use the time travel system in her Habitat to go exploring.

I was hoping she would say that.

'Future or past?" I asked.

Erimem smiled cheerfully. 'I have no idea. Yet. Do you have any suggestions?'

I tried to sound nonchalant. 'It's not my time machine,' I said. 'It's your decision.'

She just looked at me. Eyes wide in that look that says she's not taken in by the act.

'Oh, all right,' I admitted. 'I've always wanted to see the future.'

'Stay alive for a long time,' Helena said, without looking up from her copy of The Guardian. 'That way you'll see plenty of the future.'

'What's the point in having a time machine and not using it?' I asked.

'Less chance of being viciously killed,' Helena said. From the expression on her face I think it came out sharper than she intended. 'You've both been through a lot lately,' she said in a more conciliatory tone. 'I just don't like the idea of you walking into danger again,'

Erimem squeezed Helena's hand. 'We will be careful, I promise you,' she said.

Helena just snorted. 'In a pig's eye you will,' she said sourly. 'I know you two.'

'You could come with us,' Erimem suggested lightly. It was somewhere between a joke and a challenge.

Helen looked at Erimem over the top of her paper. 'I wasn't born yesterday,' she said slowly. 'And my mother didn't raise me to be mug enough to go looking for trouble.'

The kitchen door opened and Ibrahim wandered in. He had changed into jeans and a shirt that looked really comfortable. 'What are you all talking about?' he asked.

'You,' Helena replied quickly. 'And what a coward you are for not going on that run.'

Ibrahim ignored the good-natured jibe. 'I'll get my fill of sport in front of the telly. Cricket, football... god bless Sky Sports.' He smiled hopefully at Helena. 'Care to join me?'

'Sorry,' Helena answered. 'Spending the way with the girls.'

Half an hour later, Erimem and Helena were watching as I brought up the co-ordinates of the places Erimem had visited or would visit in her life. I have to admit, she gets around a bit.

Erimem looked with interest at a location far off in deep space but something closer had caught Helena's eye. 'Earth,' she said, struggling to interpret the data she was looking at. I made a mental note to make things clearer. 'Within fifty or seventy years of now.' Her eyebrows lifted thoughtfully. 'It would be interesting to see what advances have been made in medicine in that time.'

'In society in general,' I agreed. 'Have we improved at all?'

We both looked at Erimem expectantly.

'We should go and find out,' she said.

My first thought on seeing the future was 'What? Is this it?'

It looked exactly like the London we had left behind.

Only with added grunge. A lot of it.

And pissing rain. More crappy weather. Actium and here both had rain, Stalingrad had snow and freezing cold... I started to wonder if Erimem had ever been anywhere with decent weather.

It looked like we had landed in one of the crappiest parts of a big city. As a first experience of the future... underwhelming. Which makes me think... we can be over whelmed and underwhelmed... cane we just be whelmed? No idea why I thought of that.

Helena had a huge grin on her face. I wondered what was wrong with her. If she wanted weather like this all she had to do was stay put in England. Then it clicked. This was the first time she had travelled through time. It was my fourth journey and Erimem seemed to be an old hand at it. But for Helena... it was all fresh. It was exciting for her. Okay, it was exciting for all of us but this was her first time, her maiden voyage if you like. And she was loving it. Even the rain.

I was for going exploring but Erimem put a hand on my arm. She was looking up at the windows on the buildings around us and her head was tilted to the side, listening.

'What is it?' I asked.

'I do not know, but something is wrong here.' She pointed at the windows. All of them were barred or shuttered, though the shutters all looked different, like they had been made by the people living in the buildings. 'This is not a safe place,' Erimem said.

I believed her. Just along the street there were a a couple of burned out shells of cars, Blackened metal and a few melted bits of plastic were all that was left. It was like something from

Mad Max crossed with the anti-Thatcher riots of the early 80s. A lot of the houses had scorch marks as well, on the walls and especially around the doors. Somebody liked taking a light to this place.

That was a depressing thought. Half a century on, we still had arseholes who got their jollies by being complete tossers.

I thought I caught sight of somebody moving one of the shutters up on the second floor of one of the buildings but when I looked it was all still. Erimem had looked up in the same direction.

'I saw it as well,' she said.

'Somebdy's watching us?' Helena asked.

Erimem nodded. 'I believe so.'

Helena was looking at the various shutters. 'But they don't want to talk to us?'

'Or they are too afraid to do so," Erimem said softly. She forced herself to smile and glanced at me. 'I believe Andy may be so fearsome a sight that they are hiding.'

I knew she was trying to lighten the mood so I smiled. 'Been to two battles,' I said. 'Survived them both.'

Erimem started to smile but then something froze her expression.

'What is it?' I asked?

She held up her hand for quiet.

A couple of seconds later Helena spoke. 'I hear it.'

I didn't and said so. They both shushed me.

I heard it a few seconds later. The mix of an engine and shouting voices. Angry voices. A mob. It was getting closer. Jesus, I didn't like the sound of it. The closer it came, the wilder it sounded. Out of control and screaming.

'We should get away from this place,' Erimem said.

Helena agreed. 'Off the street for sure.

We hurried along the street, trying doors and windows. We could see people inside. None of them tried to help. They just cowered away from the window.

We were in trouble.

We all knew it.

The noise was getting louder. We could hear running footsteps in with the shouts and the engine. It sounded like a motorbike.

'Everything's locked,' Helena said. Her eyes kept glancing at the end of the street where the noise was coming from.

'There are people inside but they are too afraid to let us in,' Erimem said quickly. 'Whatever is coming terrifies them.'

That meant it terrified me. 'So?' I asked.

Erimem was already moving. 'We run,' she said.

The street stretched maybe fifty metres ahead of us. There were burned out wrecks of cars and assorted piles of rubbish scattered on the street – wherever this was, nobody ever cleaned here. There was no sign of anywhere to hide among that lot. The doors and windows offered nothing either.

The noises behind us were getting louder.

We kept running.

Helena had no trouble keeping up with us. She was in good shape.

The noise behind us suddenly grew louder. I risked a glance back over my shoulder. *Stupid move.* Something north of thirty men were chasing us. They were filthy. They looked wild. Not the wild look of a football crowd. Wild like they had left civilisation behind. Thrown it away. They looked like animals.

Keep running, Andy.

There was one on a motorbike. He looked worse than the rest. Bigger. He carried a Japanese sword. A katana. I could hear him screaming loudest of all. That was their leader. No doubt.

Just keep running.

The end of the street was maybe twenty metres away. We didn't know what was at the end. Whatever it was couldn't be as bad as what was behind us.

Run, Andy.

They were getting closer. I could hear them.

We got to the end of the street. To the right of us was blocked by a right-angled building so we turned left and ran.

We stopped after a few steps. It was a dead end. A blank brick wall faced us twenty metres ahead. The buildings on either side leading to the wall had the boarded over fronts of long dead shops and businesses. There was no way we could get through them.

'We can't go back,' Helena said. 'There's nowhere to hide.'

I agreed.

Erimem held up her thumb, showing the time travel ring she wore on it. 'Then we go home,' she said.

I nodded, but as we prepared to take the quick route back to 2015, one of the heavy locked doors on a business opened. A woman's voice spoke to us urgently.

'This way. Quickly.'

I would probably have twisted the ring and headed home anyway, but that's not Erimem's way. She was already running for the door. 'If it is a trap,' she called over her shoulder 'return home.'

The door led into an old shop front. It was too dark inside to see what the shop had sold. Boards nailed across the windows blocked most of the dull light from outside. All I could see was an old counter with some empty shelves.

'Follow me.' Our rescuer was already moving through to the back of the shop. 'I locked the door but if they see any sign of us they'll break it down quick enough.'

We followed her.

She led us through a door and into a small passage way that ran along the back of the shop. From there we went us a set of stairs to another short passage then down into the cellar of a building. Small openings had been knocked through between the various cellars creating an underground warren she seemed to know instinctively.

After fifteen minutes of this we were tired and dirty, with more than a few cuts and scrapes, but we were sure we had left that gang behind. The woman who had saved us led us back up above ground from a cellar into another back-shop area. From there we went upstairs, along a short passageway and then down into what looked like a soup kitchen from an old movie. Or maybe a refugee centre off the News.

There were dozens of them, mostly women or kids but there were some old people and some men there too. Rough cots were obvious in a few corners and blankets were piled around. Food was being passed out by some of the cleaner and healthier-looking women. It felt like a shelter.

Our rescuer led us through a couple of rooms, all of them with people being fed or packing away their beds.

'A sanctuary of some kind?' Erimem asked.

'Seems like it,' Helena agreed. 'It's a shelter.' Her eyes were focusing on the signs of illness and injury. She had looked at the elderly man with a broken arm and a pair of weak-looking children with sunken features and grey, lifeless skin. 'If the future's full of children with malnutrition you can stick up your arse,' she said.

'The accents are British,' I said. I waggled the time travel ring and then tapped my ear. 'These are British accents,' I said, pointing at an old woman. 'Scouser. I heard a Brummie earlier.'

'Names for people from different parts of the UK,' Helena explained for Erimem.

'I thought they were called Bloody Scousers?' Erimem said blandly.

That took Helena by surprise. 'What?'

'My fault,' I admitted. 'There was a re-run of Liverpool shagging Arsenal at Anfield a few years ago. I may have called the bloody scousers.' Well, that'll teach me to watch my mouth around somebody who's got a tendency to be literal and so soak up information. The little glint in Erimem's eyes showed she had a wicked little sense of humour.

Our rescuer led us to a smaller room. It was busy but quieter than the other rooms. There seemed to be more people working and doing the caring in here than actually in need of help. They were preparing meals, washing clothes and bed-linen by hand, getting kids dressed… the woman who had found us led us to the corner of the room where a blonde woman of about twenty five was tying a little kid's shoes. The shoes had been repaired more than once. She looked relieved when she saw us.

'You got them.' She said to our rescuer. 'Well done.'

'No worried, Angela,' the other woman replied. In this better light I could see she was younger than me. I doubt if she was twenty but she had a hard look about her face that aged her. She gave us just the slightest nod and disappeared into the shelter.

The woman she had called Angela sent the kid on his way and stood up. 'You were lucky,' she said. She wasn't condemning us or having a pop, just stating the obvious.

'We could have escaped at any time,' Erimem said with a smile. I call that her Sphinx smile. It's not genuine, just one she wears when she needs to.

'Really?' Angela did believe we could have got away on our own and we weren't for telling her how we'd do it. 'I'd like to have seen that. Razor's gang aren't kind to women who arrive here.' She smiled tightly. 'Fresh meat is a premium in here.'

'Meat?' Helena asked flatly.

Erimem was more blunt. 'You mean they eat human flesh?'

Angela smiled. It made her look really young. 'Rarely.' Her face became more serious again. 'They do much worse, believe me.'

'We do,' I said. 'I assume Razor was the guy o the bike?'

She nodded. 'His gang runs everything north of the Divide.'

'What about the police?' I asked.

She looked at me like I was an idiot. My question had genuinely shocked her. She looked around all three of us. 'That can't be a real question.'

'Why not?' Erimem asked, about a heartbeat before Helena or I could ask it.

Angela shook her head in genuine shock. 'Because everybody knows there aren't any police inside The City.'

'Not everyone,' Erimem corrected her. 'We did not know.'

'And which city?' I asked her. 'We're a little lost.'

'Everyone in The City is lost,' Angela said. She tilted her head back and smiled. 'But some of them find hope.'

I honestly didn't know what to say. It was bizarre. She looked at us with that big smile. I thought she must have been a god-botherer or something. You know the sort. When you're at your lowest ebb they tell you god will take all your problems away. They not so keen on telling you why their god gave you all this crap to deal with in the first place. It's usually 'a test' or him 'moving in mysterious ways' or even better 'it's not for us to judge god'. You know something, given the state of the world and the amount of suffering in it, and the mental behaviour he showed in the Bible, I think he really needs questioned a lot. At least I thought that when I still believed in a god. Now... I don't care what you call your magic sky pixie, I don't believe in any version of him/her/it. I really hoped we hadn't walked into some future version of those missions they had in America in the twenties and thirties.

The moment passed. I could see that both Erimem and Helena had been weirded by it too, but they didn't say anything.

'Are you saying you really don't know anything about The City?' Angela asked. 'Really?'

'Yes.' I answered patiently. 'Really.'

'Then how did you get here?'

'We were not sure exactly where we were going,' Erimem explained. It was a half truth but close enough.

Angela nodded her understanding. 'A lot of people found themselves here without knowing where they were going.' She tilted her head curiously. 'But most of them have at least heard of The City.'

'We've been off the radar for a bit,' I explained.

Apparently it didn't explain enough.

'You must have been off the planet,' Angela said.

I smiled. 'Not yet.'

She looked puzzled but shrugged it off.

Erimem interrupted. 'Tell us about The City,' she said. 'Please imagine we are completely new to the world and know nothing.'

'We get all sorts of people in here,' Angela said, 'but you would be the first aliens.' She didn't sound unkind at all. Just bemused. 'But I will tell you what you ask.'

And she did tell us. She offered us tea, which we all accepted more out of politeness than anything. Then she started to talk.

'Decades ago, the government decided that everyone in the country had to pay their way. Nobody was getting anything for nothing anymore.'

I snorted and made a comment the government we're lumbered with. I'm not a fan. I don't think Helena is either. Erimem doesn't know much about our politics yet. But I do know she doesn't trust politicians. Not a bit.

Angela ignored our comments and carried on. And what she said actually stopped me dead. I've been shocked and repelled by things that I've seen in Greece and in Stalingrad, but those were in the past or in the middle of a war. This was in the UK, and it would happen while I would still be alive.

'Faced with a struggling economy, rising unemployment and crime, and with the media full of scare stories of immigration and asylum seekers who want to steal your jobs, take your houses and do who knows what – eat your babies or something, the government put the people with nothing to work, building a city in the North to take the influx of new citizens. They built it around an old mill town. When the city was built, they kept on building, this time putting a wall around it. Once the wall was finished, they poured people in there. The unemployed, immigrants, prisoners who should have gone to jail, vagrants, the mentally ill, and some people who were just poor and hungry. They shipped them into the city and closed the wall around them.'

'They just locked their problems away?' Helena sounded angry. Really angry.

Angela shook her head. 'But they weren't finished. In the building of the city they had put cameras everywhere. Everywhere in the city was covered. At first they said it was for security. A year later they sold the cameras and their feed to a TV company. What happened in The City became an entertainment for the people lucky enough to be on the outside. On TV, on the internet, on their tablets, phones and watches. They keep up with what's happening in The City. Some of the citizens here in The City become popular. They're celebrities and have the chance to win a way out. Others became villains. The network is always coming up with new ideas. Do something to boost rating and your family get extra food for a month.'

She opened a door and pointed through into one of the bigger roims. A little globe with a red light on it was up in the corner of a wall.

'Everybody in The City is watched. I agreed to have that installed last winter when we had hundreds starving. They gave us enough food to get everyone through… just.' She sounded like accepting the camera hadn't come easy to her. 'If they have jobs – and there are enough jobs in the city to keep the pretence of a normal economy going – people are on camera as they eat their breakfast, go to work, do their jobs and come home. If they're ill, they're ill on camera. If they make love to their wives or husbands or lovers, they know a camera was pointed at them.'

Angela shut the door very softly. 'We've become a TV network's commodity in a country that had chosen to deal with its problems by turning it into a circus.' Angela smiled wryly as she finished telling the tale. 'Razor is one of the best fed people in The City,' she said. 'He murders, rapes and attacks people for no reason, but every time he does it ratings take a spike and they reward him with food or a new toy like his motorbike.

'Are there no police here?' Helena demanded. 'There must be some law.'

The way Angela looked at us you'd think we had come from a different planet. We might as well have done, I suppose.

'Don't you ever watch The City channel?' she asked. She sounded genuinely surprised. Incredulous even.

'I have never seen this channel.' Erimem answered. She carried on before Angela could ask why the hell we didn't watch this crap on TV. 'You were going to tell us about the police?'

'Pardon? Oh, right.' Erimem's sidestep pushed Angela back on track. That's a trick Erimem is very good at. 'Yes, we have police,' Angela picked up, 'but they aren't equipped to do anything. They aren't armed, they don't have the manpower. All they can do is keep themselves alive.'

'This is evil,' Erimem said flat out.

Helena shook her head, horrified by it all. 'I can't believe the government can allow this. Or the people.'

'The government makes a lot of money from The City,' Angela said quietly. 'So do the network. They pay the government a huge licence and the people subscribe for the network. Everybody profits.'

'And the people in here?' Helena asked angrily. 'She got there half a second before I did.'

'Some of us get out,' Angela answered. 'I honestly don't know if it's better on the outside than in here. We certainly have enough people volunteering to come into The City.'

'People volunteer?' I beat Helena to it this time. 'Are they mental?'

Angela shrugged. 'If the public really take to somebody in here, they can get out and make a lot of money. That's a chance some people are willing to take.'

Helena pushed her chair back noisily and stood up. She looked at Erimem and me. 'I've had enough. I think it's time for us to go.'

I agreed. Erimem looked more puzzled. She wasn't much into TV and she was a half beat behind in making sense of all of this. The looks on our faces must have known it was time to go.

'You will explain this to me later.' she said. It was part question, part demand.

'Definitely,' I agreed.

Erimem looked at Angela. 'Thank you for your hospitality and your kindness,' she said, 'but it is time for us to take our leave.'

'Where will you go?' Angela asked. 'It's dangerous out there. Especially for newcomers like you.'

Erimem smiled tightly. 'We will be in no danger, I promise you.'

Angela was going to argue. It was obvious in her expression and body language. She didn't have time. A door opened and a young woman looked in, urgently.

'What is it, Jane?' Angela asked.

The woman pointed out into the small room. 'You need to

see this.'

We all followed her through.

'What's happened?' Angela asked.

The woman just pointed at the TV. A gang – the same gang that had chased us less than an hour earlier – was gathered at building. It looked like a business of some sort. The feed switched to another camera. It was a café. Through the glass windows the staff and customers looked terrified.

'Where is that?' Angela asked. 'It looks like Ruby Square,'

The woman who had fetched us answered. 'It is.'

Angela shook her head. 'Razor's never gone so far past his own territory before. That's at least two kilometres from his boundary.'

The man on the motorcycle who had chased them earlier was clearly the leader, Razor. On screen they saw him beckon one of his lackeys forward. An overweight man with a limo and sporting a multi-coloured mullet hurried forward. He handed a bottle to Razor. Nobody thought he was interested in having a drink. He stuffed a rag into the top of the bottle and sparked a lighter at the rag's end. It took light quickly. Following Razor's lead, half a dozen other members of the gang produced their own Molotov cocktails and lit their rags.

'Home-made bombs,' I explained to Erimem. 'Whatever the liquid is, it'll be something that burns.'

She understood instantly. 'How is it you can see this happening?' Erimem asked Angela.

'Everyone in The City can see the main feeds. We don't get the indoor channel feeds, though. Not unless they want to have someone see something that could boost ratings.'

'But your police will see this?' Erimem continued. 'They must take action.'

Angela shook her head sadly. 'They might, because it's in the better part of The City but... no, they won't. They wouldn't stand a chance if they did.'

'What about the people in the café?' I asked.

Erimem finished my question. 'Do they stand a chance?'

'No,' Angel admitted miserably. 'Probably not.'

'Do you know where this place is?' Erimem demanded, staring at the TV. 'Where this is happening, I mean.'

'Of course.'

'You can take me there?'

'Well, yes.'

'Erimem, no.' Helena tried to catch Erimem's arm, but Erimem was already pushing Angela towards the door.

'What weapons do you have?'

Angela looked flustered even by the question. 'None,' she answered. 'we try to live away from the violence in here.'

'So do the people trapped in that building. Is there a way to help them?'

Everyone was looking at Angela. She knew it. I got the feeling everything in this place relied on her. Revolved around her. How much weight was that to carry? How much pressure on her shoulders? When she nodded, I was sure she did it because she didn't want to let down any of the people who were looking to her for leadership. 'I think there is.' She said, 'but it's dangerous'.

'More dangerous than being burned alive?'

'No.'

Erimem turned to Helena and me. 'Stay here. I will be back as soon as I can.' She hurried Angela away.

Helena and I exchanged a look. 'You staying here?' she asked.

'Don't be daft.'

'Nor me,' she answered sourly, hurrying after Erimem.

'Shit.' I ran after them both.

PART TWO

NO HOPE

We ran as fast as we could.

More accurately, we ran as fast as Angela could. She was young and healthy but we were faster. Even Helena. But Angela was the one who knew the route through the tunnels and side-streets to get us to the café. She moved as quickly as she could but we'd have been faster without her.

We'd also have been lost.

I kept my eyes fixed on Anna or Erimem as we ran. If I got lost… well, I had the ring on my finger. A twist of that and I would go home.

That wouldn't help those poor sods in the café though.

Through windows and occasional doors, I could see a change in the buildings. The houses were still all protected by walls and heavy doors. The difference was that it was of far better quality. This was a better area. More money.

The people still protected themselves though.

Angela was struggling. I thought of suggesting we take a minute to let her breathe. Erimem beat me to it.

'Keep going,' she demanded, aiming her words at Angela. 'Those people have little time.'

So Angela kept running.

It took another few minutes of back street, basements and houses before we were completely out in the open. The street could have been a city from my time. The stuff in shop windows was a little different but this was a proper street. Deserted but still a recognisable city centre street.

'This way,' Angela pointed along the street.

'How far?' Helena asked. She wasn't out of breath at all.

'A hundred metres or so.'

Erimem was looking around the street, absorbing every bit of information she could find. That was when it hit me that I had no idea what the hell she was planning to do – and I was absolutely sure she didn't either.

No plan, no weapons. She was winging it.

Shit.

'What is in the other buildings in the street?' Erimem demanded of Anna.

'A café, a market, a fruit shop, a really nice clothes shiop…'

'Useless,' Erimem interrupted. 'We need weapons.'

Angela shook her head vehemently. 'I don't have any weapons. I've seen what the damage they've caused to the city with people like Razor. No,' she shook her head again, 'I won't use weapons.'

I could see where she was coming from. I suppose at heart I am a pacifist. Or I'd like to be one anyway. Anybody who's sane can tell that peace is the best way forward.

In practice, life is different. In ancient Greece I got involved in a fight where people died. Same in Stalingrad. Sometimes you have to fight. You don't want to but there's no choice.

Erimem doesn't want to fight either. She prefers to find a peaceful solution. She's just more at ease when she has to accept that peaceful isn't going to work.

This was a situation when she knew peaceful wasn't going to work.

You could see her mind racing. She was thinking about every option she had. I didn't think it would take long. I didn't see any.

Erimem glanced at the buildings, looking up at the tops. 'Do you have oil here?' she asked.

'Not much. The cars are electric.'

Erimem cursed, something Egyptian. 'We have no weapons but we need to drive Razor and his warriors away.'

'Alcohol.' The word came out of my mouth before I really thought.

Erimem turned to me, an eyebrow raised. 'Oil isn't the only thing that burns,' I said. 'Alcohol, perfumes… I wasn't suggesting getting pissed.'

Erimem didn't answer me. She had already turned to Angela. 'Do you know where we can find these things?'

Angela pointed along a narrow street. 'That's the back of a restaurant and bar. They'll have alcohol.'

And Erimem was running again. I've done a hell of a lot of running since I met her. Usually in the direction opposite to the one I'd call sensible.

The back of the restaurant was open. They were throwing out rubbish. We just charged through.

'How do we burn it?' Erimem demanded.

Helena grabbed a box of napkins. 'Put these in the neck of bottles and set fire to them.'

'You are sure it will burn?'

Helena twisted the top off of a bottle and sniffed it, then set it aside. 'That won't.' The next bottle met with approval. 'Rough as boar-shit,' she said wrinkling her nose.

I took a sniff. I could almost feel the layers of skin inside my nose blistering. 'Home made?' I asked.

'There are no rules on who makes alcohol in the city,' Angela explained. 'At least none that are enforced. It's left for people to work it out. Some of it is pretty rough. That's one of the reasons I don't touch it.'

'The other reasons?' I asked.

She smiled wryly. 'For some reason I have become well known, inside the city and on the outside. They think I'm…' She paused and looked embarrassed. 'They think I'm one of the nice ones in here.'

'A hero?'

She laughed, but without any humour. 'They need villains to boost their ratings. That means they turn others into heroes, whether we want to be or not.'

'And that increases your chances of getting out of here?'

'If I leave, what happens to the people here who need help?'

I studied at her for a moment. 'You've had the chance to

leave, haven't you?'

Again that wry smile. 'I never claimed to be bright.'

I didn't have time to answer. Erimem and Helena were pulling a couple of crates of the foul smelling rot-gut onto a table. She was brisk, talking like we were her army. 'We need to go onto the roof.'

I didn't argue. I just followed her.

At least getting to the roof was easy. Stairs at the back led all the way up. We carried a case between two of us. That case us thirty bottles. On the roof, Erimem spaced us out. She took the corner above the café herself.

We could hear the gang below. Razor was revving his bike's engine. Somebody fired a few gunshots and screams followed quickly. That was enough for Erimem. She leaned over the wall and peered down at the gang. We were a couple of storeys up, maybe fifty feet.

'Leave this place,' she shouted. 'Leave or I will kill you all.'

Most of the gang looked around, trying to find where the voice had come from. A couple looked up and saw Erimem. They started laughing. That spread to the rest of the gang when they realised who was talking. One of the gang aimed a gun but the leader waved a hand to stop him.

'You're going to kill us from up there?' he shouted. 'Come down and talk about it.'

'I will come down when you are gone and these people have peace,' she shouted back.

'You'll come down when I tell you.' He indicated for a couple of his gang to come for Erimem.

She flicked a wrist sending one bottle over the side. It hit the pavement and erupted into flames in front of the two gang members. They dived backwards.

'I told you to leave,' Erimem repeated. 'This is not your

place in this city.'

'Get her,' Razor shouted. 'Nobody kill her.'

Erimem sent another bottle down. That smashed and sent flames all around Razor. She nodded an instruction for the rest of us to start throwing. Helena had found matches in the bar, so we lit the napkins and threw the bottles.

I should have felt guilty. There was a chance I'd kill someone. But I wasn't thinking about that. All I thought was that we might protect people. I lobbed the bottles towards the edges of the gang. Helena didn't. She threw with all her strength straight into the heart of the gang. One of her bottles smashed on the head of a member of the gang. He was drenched in the rot-gut and on fire and on fire in seconds. The sight of one of their friends burning sent the gang into panic and they started to scatter. Helena threw another bottle. This one hit the ground between two gang-members. The splashes of burning liquid caught the legs of those two gang members. I heard their screams as their legs took light. The gang was scattering and starting to run. Erimem and Helena kept throwing. More members of the gang were hit by burning liquid and tried to put out the flames as they ran. Erimem's last bottle landed just behind Razor's back wheel and engulfed the back of his bike in fire before the gang were out of range.

We stayed in place until it was clear that the gang had really gone. I had no idea what we'd do if they did come back. Both Erimem and Helena were out of bottles and I had only one left. Then I saw Angela's clutch of bottles. They were all still intact. She hadn't thrown any. She was shaking. Badly. She was terrified. Really terrified.

'I didn't throw…'

'Smart move,' I said, interrupting her. 'You kept some in reserve in case we needed them. Good thinking.'

That was horse-shit and we both knew it. She had frozen. I didn't blame her. I'd been terrified, too. It's just that I've seen

29

enough now to keep me moving when things get rough.

Erimem was already heading for the stairs. 'We should see if anyone is hurt.'

By the time we reached the street, Angela had composed herself. The street was covered with broken glass and the last flames of the burning booze. It smelled like the worst off-licence in the world had exploded.

On the other hand, the gang was gone.

People had started to emerge from doors and look out of windows. The people began coming out of the cafe as well. One of them had been shot in the arm. It didn't look bad but hat do I know about gunshot wounds? I guessed it was a random shot from the gang and this poor sod had just been unlucky. Wrong place, wrong time. IN the distance I could hear a couple of sirens getting louder.

Better late than never.

It turned out there were three sirens. The police arrived and started to take statements, though they admitted they had seen most of it on TV. I hadn't noticed them before but the lamp-posts and buildings all had cameras, which had been covering what was happening in the street. There had even been a camera inside the café, trained on the guy who had been shot. I heard some of the locals saying they had been watching on the blue button, with a doctor giving an update on how long the guy had before he bled out.

I couldn't get my head around that. They weren't just part of the show. They were part of the audience too. I just didn't get that.

Thankfully, the second siren was an ambulance and they started tending to the patient straight away. The third siren… that was a TV crew. Everybody moved aside for them. Even the police got out of the way. The doctor was asking the patient questions. How he felt, if his vision was okay… the TV mob just shoved him out of the way and started asking the shot guy questions. How did he feel? Was he afraid he was going to die? Had the doctor given a prognosis? Was he going to recover?

The worst thing was – he answered. He didn't just answer, he looked happy to answer. And I understood why. This was his time, his fifteen minutes of fame. Somebody had put a bullet in him but that was his opportunity to get his face in front of the camera. He was playing it so brave, and trying too hard. I wanted to slap him and tell him to get some dignity.

What right did I have to think that way? Who knows what kind of life that poor bastard lived? I had no idea what had dragged him into the city in the first place. I didn't know his story. I had no right to judge him.

The reporter was a pushy blonde woman with teeth that were too perfect and make-up that was sharp rather than attractive. She reminded me of the people on TV that I never watch. The ones I always switch off. The ones with ambition but no talent. The reporter was looking round. She touched a finger to her ear, obviously listening to someone on an earpiece. Immediately she lost interest in the victim. She cut the interview off quickly. This ordinary bloke, who just took a bullet for no reason was being turfed aside. He wasn't interesting enough.

The Reporter made a bee-line for Angela, pushing a microphone at her. 'Angela, the city's famous Angel of Mercy, tell us what happened. Why have you suddenly chosen to face violence with violence? You've always avoided confrontation before.'

'We had to save these poor people,' Angela said. 'They were going to be killed. We had to do something to help them.'

Angela's voice caught me by surprise. It had just too much sincerity in it.

The Reporter hadn't noticed. She ploughed on. 'And you chased away Razor's gang all by yourself?'

'Oh, no. There were four of us. Four women against that entire gang, but what could we do? We had to help or the people trapped in the café would have been killed.'

Jesus. She'd been shitting herself up on the roof, too scared to throw a Molotov Cocktail but she was playing a role in front of the cameras.

'How did you come up with your plan?' the reporter asked.

'We didn't have any weapons so we had to improvise.'

'Do you think Razor will target you even more than he has already?'

Angela shrugged. 'I don't see how he can. He already dominates our part of the city. The important thing is that the people in this part of the city are safe.'

The reporter pressed her ear again. 'I'm hearing that in our instant-poll to decide the hero of the day, you scored ninety three percent to the victim's seven.'

'We're not heroes,' Angela said. The modesty was about as genuine as a politician's smile. 'We just did what we had to do.'

'Your personal approval rating has gone up to ninety six.'

Angela smiled just a little, as if she was embarrassed. 'I just hope we can help some people.'

The reporter nodded. 'You always do. And this time, you earned a Class One drop of luxury food.'

Angela squeezed the reporter's arm. 'Thank you. Thank you so much. You have no idea how much that will mean to so many people in this city.'

The reporter swung the microphone to Erimem. 'Do you have anything to say about what happened?'

Erimem looked at the reporter, Angela and then around the scene. 'The injured man must be tended,' she said. She spun around and walked away, leaving Angela to cover for her abruptness.

An hour later we were sitting back in the shelter where we had been taken first.

'All right,' Angela said, looking at us in turn. 'You must think I'm an absolute monster for taking the credit for your idea and for saving those men,'

'I do not actually care,' Erimem said coolly, 'but I am interested in why you chose to do so.'

Angela leaned forward. 'Because you're new,' she said. 'And if someone new did what we did… well, that would lift your approval ratings but not enough to trigger a drop of food into the city, and we need that food desperately. Razor's gang has stolen so much that we have people starving. This will save them.' She sighed. 'I hate the game I have to play with the cameras, but it keeps people alive, so all I can ask is that you please accept my apologies and understand.'

Erimem thought for a moment before speaking. 'I understand your actions, she said. 'In your position I would have done no different. When we lead, we must always put the needs of those who follow us ahead of our own needs. I bear no ill will.'

'I'm glad.' She looked at Erimem with interest. 'You sound like you have been a leader. You're young to be a politician.'

'I led my country once,' Erimem answered. 'Long ago. Much longer than you would imagine.'

'And yet you're here now?'

'Life is full of surprises,' I cut in, sparing Erimem the explanation.

She smiled her thanks. 'When will the food arrive?'

'Tomorrow morning.' Angela yawned hugely. 'Oh, I'm sorry. Listen, we should get some sleep. It'll be a busy day tomorrow. I'll have Diane show you to some beds.'

I glanced at Erimem. The question in my eyes was obvious. *Are we staying?*

Erimem smiled gratefully. 'Thank you,' she said. 'You are

very kind.'

We were shown to a sort of dormitory. Four cots in one small room. Again, it reminded me of something I'd expect to have seen in 1930s Chicago during the Depression and Prohibition. The bedclothes were clean but threadbare. My guess was it would be a chilly night.

'Why are we staying?' I asked Erimem. 'We got rid of the gang. We even blagged some extra food for people here.'

'Blagged?'

'Obtained,' Helena explained quickly.

'So?' I asked. 'Why are we still here?'

'Do you wish to return to your own time?' Erimem asked.

'Of course I do… but I'm guessing there's a reason you want to stay here tonight?'

Erimem wrinkled her nose. 'I do not like this place or time.'

'So we're staying why exactly?'

'I wish to make sure that the food arrives with those who need it.'

I could see where she was going. 'You think Razor will try to steal it?'

She nodded. 'We injured him yesterday. He was embarrassed publicly. A leader who rules by fear cannot survive if he displays that kind of weakness. He will try to take the food in the morning.'

'And we're going to stop him?'

She nodded.

'How exactly?'

Erimem smiled. 'That is what we must discuss before we go to sleep.'

The drop was set for a sort of railway platform. The train came in deep underground and only emerged to come in at the platform. There were elven of them scattered around the city. To keep raiders off guard, the drop location wasn't revealed until an hour before it happened. The problem was that the drops always happened within a certain distance of the home of the people receiving it, which usually narrowed the decision down to a maximum of three. Erimem offered a plan that was simple enough. Once she knew which station the food was coming in, Angela should send a group of people to a different station and make it look like they would be collecting the food there. A simple diversion. Once that was done, get the food into small vans and scatter, distributing it quickly. It wasn't rocket science but it would do.

At ten o'clock, Angela was informed by the network of which platform was being used. On cue, she sent a group of her people to another platform four miles east of the genuine location. We waited fifteen minutes before heading to where the food was really coming in. Angela had said that the hostel was always watched by one of Razor's gang. She also guessed that Razor would pull his men from scouting if they were going to have a raid.

We went underground and through back streets until we clambered into a couple of vans. Twenty minutes later we were going through a fearsome looking set of gates. The signs said they were electrified and that the compound was protected by motion sensitive machine guns. Suddenly the Underground at rush hour wasn't such a bad proposition. In total there were ten vans. They came from all different directions and were all about the size of a Transit.

The platform was built for cargo, not for passengers. There were no amenities, no seats. Just a few automatic forklift type machines. The train arrived exactly on time. Heavy gates which barred access to the tunnel dropped down into the ground ten seconds before the train came through.

The unloading was quick and efficient. The forklifts moved palates of boxes with a remorseless sort of efficiency. The whole thing took ten minutes tops. As soon as the last door closed at the backs of the Transits, I waved to Erimem. She had insisted on us posting lookouts to make sure Razor's gang didn't catch us by surprise. She called to the other lookouts – including Helena – and they ran back to the vans.

The vans scattered as soon as they left the little enclosure. Each one was going to a different part of Angela's neighbourhood. Scattering made sure there was no way Razor's gang could grab all of the food, even if they caught up with any of us.

As it turned out, we were in the last of the vans to leave. Six turned right. I could see them taking different routes, two taking an immediate left and four going ahead. They'd each take a different path and they wouldn't stop for anything.

The last fourturned left. We were at the back. The lead two went straight on. The one just in front of us had Angela as a passenger. We'd travel with her about three quarters of the way before going to different streets.

We took a left, then a right. The streets were quiet, no sign of trouble. I started to relax.

I should have known better.

A truck hurtled out of a side road and slammed into the side of the van with Angela in it. The van slid sideways before being thrown onto its side. It skidded along the road and smashed through the front of a shop. Our driver tried to slow us down but there was no time. He yanked the wheel to the side and we clipped the back of the truck. We spun out of control and crashed hard into a wall. The seatbelt dug hard into my chest, my shoulder, forcing the air from my body. I tried to move but I couldn't. Helena was trying to move as well. She just moaned. Erimem's face was a red mask. She had a cut somewhere in her scalp. The window on her side was broken and I saw glass in her hair. Her head was tilted at an angle. I thought her neck was broken but she was breathing. I tried to move again and managed to twist my head. The driver hadn't been so lucky. His head flopped on a broken neck and the wheel had crushed his chest.

I tried to release the seatbelt but my hands wouldn't listen to my brain. My head started to throb and then the pain in my chest really hit. I heard myself whimper with the pain.

There was movement outside. It took a second for me to recognise them.

Razor's gang.

I forced my head to twist so I could see better. Razor was at the other van. Its windscreen was a mass of cracks but it hadn't broken. He kicked it twice, shattering it, before reaching inside. He hauled Angela out by the hair. She was limp, not moving. It looked like she was dead. But then her arm moved slightly. He hauler her upright by the hair and hurled her towards a couple of his gang. They caught her before she could fall and dragged her away. He waved to another of his gang, who came forward.

Christ, no.

He was holding bottles, the same as had thrown at them yesterday. Razor laughed and nodded. The first bottle hit the overturned van and took flame instantly.

He lit the second bottle fuse and looked at us good and hard before throwing it straight at the cab of our van.

PART THREE

NO MERCY

The bottle hit the front of our truck. It shattered and the liquid caught fire instantly. It wasn't the cheap booze we had used. I recognised the smell.

Petrol.

I struggled. I was desperate and that forced my body to move. The pain in my shoulder and chest was forgotten. Panic blanked it out. I pulled ask the seatbelt and scrabbled to get it free.

The flames had taken hold of the front of the truck. I could smell that sick stench of rubber burning. The tyres were on fire. The flames were on the other side of the windscreen. I could feel the heat. The windshield wouldn't last much longer. I struggled harder to free my seatbelt.

There was a scream from outside. It was Angela. Razor was dragging her away. The gang was getting out of there before the truck exploded.

I struggled harder but I couldn't release the damn seatbelt.

'I've got it.'

I looked at Helena, shocked. 'We've got to get out of here.'

She ignored me, pushed my hands away from the seatbelt and twisted it. The belt came free. She quickly released first Erimem's seatbelt and then her own. She pulled Erimem away from the door. Black smoke and flames belched along that side of the truck.

'We can't get out that side,' she said. 'Open the other side.'

'But…' Our driver was between me and the door and the wheel and been pushed forward into his chest. We couldn't move him. Climbing over him was horrible,. It felt wrong but what else could we do? I managed to get the door open and more or less fell out. I caught door handle just in time to avoid falling on my face and probably breaking my neck.

The black smoke and the heat yanked the air out of my lungs and I started choking.

'Grab Erimem.' Helena was half pushing, half dragging

Erimem's unconscious body out of the door. I caught Erimem's shoulders and pulled her down. Helena jumped out a second later.

'We need to get away from here,' I said.

Helena nodded and we each took one of Erimem's arms and dragged her away. We hauled her behind a pillar just in time. Ten seconds later whatever fuel cell powered the van went up and I slumped to the ground beside Erimem.

My sense of direction is pretty good. Helena's is obviously much better. Once Erimem had started to come round, Helena led us through the streets to an abandoned shop she recognised as having an entrance to the underground network of passages. We followed her.

I was worried about Erimem. She hadn't said much since we explained what had happened. Helena wanted to examine her but she knew we needed to be off the streets before she did that.

When we eventually lurched back into Angela's shelter, we didn't have to explain to anyone what had happened. It had all been on TV. The cameras had seen it all. Everyone had seen the attack on our vans and Angela being taken.

The atmosphere in the Shelter was awful. They were convinced Angela was dead. Some of them just hoped she was. None of us had any doubts that there were much worse things than death that Razor and his gang could do to a lone woman.

The TV channel was rerunning the incident over and over again. Commentators were dissecting it. A doctor was discussing what she thought Erimem's injury was likely to be. A vote scrolled along the bottom of the screen, encouraging viewers to vote on whether Angela was alive or dead. 785 said she was dead.

Helena looked at the screen with disgust before turning her attention back to Erimem. Her eyes were less glassy than they had been and she was more focused on what was going on around her. She answered Helena's questions with short answers but they were clear and precise.

Helena dabbed away the blood from Erimem's scalp and peered at the cut, partly hidden by Erimem's black hair. 'You got lucky,' she said. 'You're dazed but you avoided a concussion. God only knows how. This cut probably should get stitched but I don't have what I need for that here.' She rummaged through the first aid supplies she had demanded when we got back. She smeared a glob of white gel onto Erimem's scalp. Our friend winced but said nothing. 'Petroleum jelly. It'll help control the bleeding.'

Erimem pulled herself up to her feet and twisted her neck and shoulders, testing to see how much she hurt. From the look on her face I'd say she hurt a lot. She rubbed her shoulder gingerly and tried to lift the arm. She winced again.

'It's bruised, not broken,' Helena said. 'But it's going to hurt like hell for a few days.'

Erimem nodded and walked over to the TV. They were replaying the attack on our vans yet again. They had another angle of us crawling out of the vans. Christ, we were a mess. They had new angles of Razor dragging Angela away as well. She looked terrified. There was a lot of blood on her and she was struggling to walk properly. Her legs buckled at one point. Razor kept a tight grip on her hair and hauled her back to her feet. He threw her across the front of his bike and the gang took off. A sidebar slid in on the right:

ANGEL
OF
MERCY
DEAD?

The words slid up to allow more text to appear.

ANGELA MURDERED?
SPECIAL DISCUSSION PROGRAMME TONIGHT

'Where would they take her?' Erimem asked the room.

Nobody answered. They didn't even look at her. They were still shocked and terrified of what had happened – and what might still happen.

'Has the gang been seen since this?' I asked. 'Have they done anything? Made any kind of statement?'

Erimem looked at me, slightly confused, then she nodded. 'Everything here is about show.'

Helena had joined us. 'Whatever they do to Angela, they'll do it on camera.'

'For the ratings,' I agreed.

The picture changes abruptly, switching a presenter in a studio. She was trying to hide her excitement – but not trying very hard. 'We have just received a communication from Razor's gang.' She stopped, tilted her head, obviously listening to an ear-piece. 'The message is a video from Razor himself. Here it is.'

The picture switched. The studio was replaced by a room strewn with junk and in the broadcaster's stead Razor stood staring at the camera. It was the first time I'd seen him clearly. He was certainly the tallest of the gang, and the broadest. He would have been a good looking man, I suppose, if his life hadn't taken its toll on him. His nose had been broken at least once and tilted to the side. The left side of his face was pitted and livid, the sign of being burned years before, with a scar running down the middle of the burned tissue.

'The woman, Angela, is alive,' he said. 'At least for…' he checked a wristwatch theatrically, 'another two hours. At six o'clock we will bring her to Beaton Square. We'll kill her live, in front of every one of you.' He smiled. It was a horrible sight.

Just vicious. He enjoyed what he was doing. 'You will see the blood of an angel. If the police try to interfere we will hunt them down and kill every one of them. When we kill the angel, the city belongs to us. Everybody will pay us a fee. A fee for using our streets, a fee for running a business, a fee for using the transport... we're the law here now. It's Razor's Law – do as I tell you or you die.'

The screen faded to black for a long moment before cutting back to the studio. The presenter started talking fast. 'Of course, we will have full live coverage of the events at Beaton Square tonight. In twenty minutes, at the turn of the hour we will be talking with a psychiatrist about the ordeal being endured by Angela.' She paused, listening to her earpiece. A message flashed up on the screen:

ANGELA FATALITY BETTING SUSPENDED

The presenter picked up her report, her voice full of excitement. 'And not for the first time ever we have a reporter inside the hostel Angela has run for the past number of years.'

I looked at Erimem and Helena, wondering what the hell that vacuous cow was talking about. We were in the hostel she was talking about. Then we saw her. Actually we heard her first. The same bitch who had been on the spot at the attack on the café. She was striding through the hostel with a cameraman in tow, keeping her squarely in the picture.

'Handing over to our reporter, Denise, now,' the presenter said, and then the picture switched to the camera's live feed from inside the hostel.

The reporter, Denise, stuck her microphone under the nose of a teenage girl, who was crying. 'How do you feel knowing that Angela is going to be murdered?' The girl just cried – and the cow kept the microphone in her face. 'Do you have any last words about Angela?' the reporter carried on. The girl shook her head.

Denise, the reporter, carried on. 'You can see how much Angela means to the people here. There is a terrible atmosphere in the shelter, an air of fatality. These people have given up hope.'

Erimem snapped, 'Have you no respect?'

Denise ignored the question. I wished Erimem hadn't said anything. Engaging with this bitch in any way, even to call her out on being an evil cow, was doing what she wanted. She needed attention to keep the story going. 'You're one of the people who were in the other van, aren't you?'

'What does that matter?' Erimem demanded flatly.

'How badly are you hurt? You were the one who was bleeding when they pulled you out of the van.' She turned to her cameraman. 'Try to get a look at her wound.'

Erimem glared at the cameraman. 'If you move any nearer I will smash your machine and force the broken pieces down your throat.'

He held back. *Smart boy.*

The reporter wasn't giving up though. 'Who are you? We haven't seen much of you before. What's your name?'

'My name is my business and none of your concern.' Erimem waved a dismissive hand at the reporter. 'Now leave us alone.'

'The public want to know,' the reporter argued. 'They have a right to know.'

This time I was the one who answered angrily. I know I shouldn't have. I should have kept my big fat mouth shut but she had made me so angry. 'What we think is our business. Nobody's got a right know a bloody thing we don't want them to and you don't have any right to stick your camera in people's faces when they're worried about their friend.'

'The public has a right to know everything that happens in the City.' She sounded so smug and superior I wanted to flatten the bitch. 'The laws of the City are clear. The public have a right to know everything.'

'From what I have seen, the people of this city have little respect for any of its laws,' Erimem snapped.

I added, 'She's saying you can stick your laws up your arse.'

The bitch didn't answer straight away. I'm pretty sure I heard a tinny voice in her ear. 'Angela is to be executed in just a few hours,' she said, relaying whatever her producer was shouting at her. 'Where do you intend to watch it?'

'We will not be watching,' Erimem said coldly. 'Because she will not be killed. Your machine relays my image, yes?' Denise nodded. 'Then I send a message to Razor and I make him this promise. If he harms Angela, I will kill him. I will cut the entrails from his body and feed them to dogs while he still breathes. If he takes this woman's life, his own is forfeit.'

With that she pushed past Denise and went through a door into our dormitory. Helena and I followed her through. The last thing I heard before I closed the door was Denise talking to her cameraman.

'Just tell me you got that.'

'And the point of that was?' Helena asked Erimem almost as soon as the door was closed. 'You said earlier that his authority came from people knowing he'd carry out threats. He can't back off from killing her now.'

'I know,' Erimem answered quickly, 'but it also means he will not kill her before the stated time. He will want to be seen carrying out his threat exactly as he promised.'

Helena still didn't look convinced. 'That hasn't bought us – or her – much time.'

Erimem smiled tightly, without any humour. 'I know. But it gives us time to find Razor's lair.'

I stared at her. 'How the hell are we going to do that?'

'With that.' Erimem pointed at a computer in the corner. 'If

47

that… hyena out there was able to find a place as secret as this, then they must also know where Razor's den is. Use the computer to find it.'

'Is that all?' I shook my head. 'Have you any idea how complicated that will be?'

'You understand these machines,' she argued.

'I understand them in our time,' I shot back. 'Christ knows how much they'll have changed since my day.'

'There is no option.'

She was right. We were painted into a corner and I didn't see any alternative. 'Shit.'

As it turned out, computers hadn't changed all that much. The surface was different – interface was buy voice command and so on, but a lot of the basic logic and structure of the system was the same. I was able to get online and access streaming cameras pretty quickly. I caught at least one that I wish I hadn't seen. Digging deeper, I got to a problem pretty quickly. There were a set of feeds that were password protected. 'I can't access them,' I told Erimem.

She looked frustrated. 'Would anyone here have a password?'

'Doubt it,' I answered. 'We're on the lowest rung of society here.'

'What about the reporter?' Helena asked. 'Her network runs this lot. She'll need some kind of password to log in, surely?'

'Probably,' I agreed, 'but she's not likely to cough it up to us, is she?'

'No, but we might catch it if they had to log in again.'

As plans go, the best we came up with was ridiculously simple, and it actually worked. The camera's battery pack was external and easy to replace. In passing the cameraman, Helena nudged him slightly – and jostled his camera a lot. She apologised, he said it was no problem because he hadn't been filming, the had a chat for a minute or so and when he was called on to film, he cursed, and realised he had to log in again.

'Username: F. Gibney; password: Woodstock,' Helena said as she came back into the dormitory.

The network accepted the log in first time and we were into the pass protected area.

'Shit,' I muttered. 'There must be two hundred of them.'

'Then we must begin quickly,' Erimem said. I think my expression must have given away what I thought about that. 'And perhaps that was stating the obvious,' she said wryly. 'I apologise.'

I waved away the apology. 'No need. I'll get started.'

I started scanning the protected feeds. Some of them were far too dull to merit having a camera aimed at them – store rooms, locked gateways, empty roads... I flicked through them quickly. After more than sixty we finally found something interesting. There was a warehouse of some kind. Sitting inside was Razor's motorbike. A couple of his men looked like they were standing guard. I scanned the naming structure for other feeds. Eight or nine were clearly linked. I cycled through them. A few of his men playing cards, one of them lying drunk on a bed... and then we got it.

Razor and Angela.

Just the two of them, sitting in a small room at a battered old table. He was huge. He just dwarfed her. She was talking fast and she was really animated. She had to be begging for her life. He didn't look bothered. No matter how much she talked, he just wasn't giving much back.

'Can we hear what they are saying?' Erimem asked. 'We may learn something from what she is saying.'

Being honest, I didn't want to hear what she was saying. I didn't need to hear her begging for her life. I didn't want to hear him gloating about how he was going to kill her. I didn't want any of that, but Erimem was right. Helena knew it too.

She nodded at me sadly.

'We have to hear it.'

So I turned up the sound.

An hour later I was still sitting at the computer. Erimem and Helena had gone. I was left on computer duty. It made sense for me to stay. I knew the computer system better than either of them – meaning I knew a little bit about it while they knew absolutely bugger all. What's the old saying? In the land of the blind, the one eyed man is king? I was the best option we had.

That didn't mean I had to like it.

On the other hand, I was getting the hang of using the cameras to track Erimem and Helena's progress. Communicating with them wasn't easy. Our phones didn't work, so all I could do was use the camers in there are to pass rudimentary messages. If things were safe I'd swing the camera up and down like a nod. If there was a problem I'd move it from side to side, like I was shaking my head. Like I said, it wasn't great but it was all we could manage.

Every now and then, Erimem would stop at a camera and ask me questions. *Was there a crowd heading for the square? Was there any sign of Angela or Razor? Were the police going to do anything?* She asked her questions and I replied, then they moved on.

One of the odd things I noticed was that Erimem and Helena ran in a very similar way. They weren't all pumping knees and arms. They were economical and used as little effort as possible.   When I was at school, I ran. I was good too. Maybe I'd have been better than good if I ran the way they did. Or maybe they'd move faster if they ran my way.

Or maybe I was just trying to distract myself from thinking about what was going to happen.

They were on the last part of their journey. A couple of hundred metres from where they were going. They dipped out of sight for half a minute as they crossed a patch of rubble, and I breathed easier as I picked them up on the far side. I know Erimem is a warrior and she can take care of herself. She's small but she's been trained. She can take down men twice her size. Helena's a doctor. She saves lives, she doesn't get into fights. Erimem is her friend, too, and I know she sees Erimem as family because Erimem and Ibrahim are related. Still… is that a good enough reason for her to risk her life? I suppose it must be. We always look out for family and friends.

They cut along a side street. It was more or less empty bar a few people hurrying home. I guessed they wouldn't want to miss the excitement on TV. There was an abandoned restaurant on the corner. They stopped in the doorway just ahead of the restaurant and pressed themselves back against the door. They waited a few minutes and then they twitched as they heard the restaurant's door open. They didn't move, keeping out of sight until after a small figure had emerged. Two much larger figures followed her. Angela, with two of Razor's gang as her guards.

Erimem and Helena waited until the Angela and her guards had passed before rushing from cover. They hit the two members of the gang hard. Erimem kicked hard at the knee of the guard nearest to them. His leg buckled and he went down to one knee. Erimem ignored him and attacked the second of the guards. She had pulled small lead pipes from inside her jacket and swung them hard. One smashed into the man's arm, the other cracked off his jaw. He dropped, unconscious, blood spraying from his face. She turned back to the first gang member in time to see Helena Club him down with a broken brick. She hit him on the side of the neck and he dropped to the ground. Helena checked his neck and said something to Erimem. Looked like she was confirming that the man was still alive.

They both looked around quickly, ensuring that nobody else was with Angela and then hurried to her. She was staring at them in shock. Her hands weren't tied. Erimem and Helena each took an arm and hurried her away along the street, heading back the way they had come. I kept them under surveillance as they followed twists and turns through the streets. We used the same yes/no code to make sure they were going in the right direction. I could see that Angela was asking questions. They were answering quickly, without taking time to give her too much detail. They were running. They'd need their breath for that.

After a few minutes we started to see more people in the streets. They were all heading in one particular direction. Erimem and Helena kept Angela moving. She was starting to look uncomfortable. I wasn't surprised. Some of the crowd recognised her. She really started to look uncomfortable as the crowd got thicker, but both Erimem and Helena kept a grip on her. Erimem had a plan and we didn't expect Angela to like it much.

They weren't heading back to the hostel. Instead, they were heading for Beaton Square, where Razor was due to kill her. She had to be wondering what the hell they were doing. Why were they taking her to the place Razor was going to be?

To be honest, Erimem's plan scared the shit out of me, too. And I was stuck at a computer miles away from the square.

They stuck with the crowd and tried to blend in as they got to Beaton Square. The crowd was big, definitely in the thousands. The square was a decent size. Not Trafalgar Square big but a decent size, with screens on two of the sides, which seemed to be the way of things here. A platform made of wooden crates had been built in the middle. Razor was standing on it, surrounded by a bunch of his men. They were all carrying weapons of some sort. Razor himself was looking around the people.

They belonged to him now.

That was what he was thinking. They had all come to see

him take complete control of the city. For some reason I thought of footage from the Second World War, of the French watching the Germans march into Paris. It had that sense of unavoidable horror about it.

Razor had a microphone of some sort. I guessed it was one of those Madonna jobs, the kind that were stuck to the face. I hope it was stuck to his burned skin so it would hurt more when it came off.

'Where's Angela?' His voice sounded loud and angry. 'Bring her here.'

Nobody moved.

'Bring her to me.' He looked around the square, and eventually held his gaze at a small side street which led onto the Square. 'Where is she?'

'Not where you expect.' The microphones built into the camera gear picked up Erimem's voice.

The crowd rumbled as she nimbly climbed up onto the platform.

Razor's head tilted. She was unexpected but you could see his brain working. Was she a threat or an opportunity? 'And what do you know about it?' he asked.

Erimem made a great show of being unimpressed by Razor or any of his gang but she was intelligent enough to keep her distance. 'I am one of the ones who rescued her from your men,' she answered loudly. That got a real reaction from the crowd. Angela was safe? She had escaped?

We knew it would be a positive reaction. A couple of them started cheering.

'She escaped?' Razor yelled.

'She was rescued,' Erimem corrected the thug. 'By and friend and I.'

'Really?'

'Yes, really.'

Razor examined Erimem for a long moment. 'Have you

53

come here to take her place?'

'You think I have come here to be killed?' she asked. 'You are a very foolish man.'

'For that I'll definitely kill you in Angela's place.' He sounded like he was looking forward to that.

'You are a very dull man,' Erimem said, dripping scorn. 'And you are not as intelligent as you claim to be. '

'Is that a fact?'

'Yes,' Erimem said blithely. 'You have not noticed that Angela is actually here.' She wave her hand briskly in a short signal and Helena vaulted up onto the platform. A few moments later, a nervous-looking Angela climbed up beside them. The crowd roared at that.

'You came back?' Razor sounded shocked. 'That's not clever.'

Angela pointed at Erimem. 'She said I would be safe. She said there were sights trained on you.'

Razor stiffened. 'She said what?'

Erimem held up a hand and smiled secretively. 'I have to admit that was not exactly true.'

'What?'

Erimem continued, 'There are no guns aimed at you at this time…'

Razor squared his shoulder. 'And you called me stupid.'

Erimem continued, '…however cameras were aimed at you when you are Angela were talking in your base.'

'What?'

Angela caught Helena's arm and obviously asked the same question.

Erimem ignored the question. 'But if you do not believe me, see for yourself.'

That was my cue. I hit ENTER and played the video I'd pulled from the network's protected archive.

On the screens in the square, and on every screen that had

tuned in for the show, the image changed from the square to the sight of Razor and Angela sitting at the table in his shitty lair. Sadly, I turned the sound to maximum.

Razor was speaking. 'Are you sure it will work?'

Angela nodded. 'Of course it will. When I escape on my way to Square, the public will give me so much support.'

'It'll make me look weak,' Razor protested. 'I said I'd kill you.'

'But there will be hundreds at the square,' Angela said patiently. 'Killing as many of them as you like will make you look stronger than killing an innocent defenceless woman like me.'

Razor snorted. 'You almost kept a straight face when you said 'innocent and defenceless'.'

'Almost,' Angela agreed.

I paused the video as we had agreed I would. Erimem started talking.

'Angela and Razor have had an understanding for many years. They have played roles in this city for years. The threat from Razor has made Angela the greatest hero in the city. Her reaction to Razor has made him the greatest threat here.'

I hit ENTER again. Another video played, a later part of Angela's conversation with Razor.

'Our arrangement has worked for years,' Angela said.

Razor cut across her. 'For both of us.'

Angela nodded. 'A good hero needs a strong villain. This is good business for both of us.'

I killed the feed.

Erimem looked from Razor to Angela and back again. 'You have manipulated the people of this city, and the network knew you were doing it. They allowed you to do as you wished in order to protect their ratings. They have allowed you to lie to people here and to use them for your own ends.' She turned to Angela, and fixed her with a disgusted look. 'You, in particular, are guilty of allowing people to be injured and killed, while pretending to care.' She shook her head angrily. 'You disgust me even more than that.' She pointed a finger at Razor.

Razor was looking at the crowd around his platform. The mood had changed. Some had arrived with curiosity, others ready to be seen to be close to the new power in the city, others had simply been too afraid not to come. Now they were angry. You could hear it. Their voices were growing louder.

Erimem spoke again, louder to be heard over the noise. 'The people of this city have a chance now to remove the people who have deceived them. If they choose, your time here is over.'

Angela looked terrified. She deserved to. The people in the square all had that same disgusted disappointed expression we had worn when we first saw the footage. She knew it was finished. Razor was different. His reaction was always going to be for violence. He raised his gun and fired into the crowd, trying to show he was in control. Erimem moved fast, slamming one of the metal pipes she was carrying down on Razor's wrist. The bone must have shattered under the impact and he dropped the weapon. The crowd was already on the move surging towards the platform. The last thing I saw before the crowd engulfed the platform was Erimem and Helena dropping off the raised surface down into the crowd.

I pulled the plug on the feed, killing the link to every house in the city and then I started deleting files and pathways, taking the network apart. It took me twenty minutes to do all the damage I could with the clearance we'd stolen. By the time I was done, the network's system was a mess. They would probably be able to repair it but they wouldn't do it quickly. By the time it was over, things would be different in the city. I had just finished when Erimem and Helena arrive in the shelter. There was a question I had to ask.

'Are they dead?'

'I do not know.' Erimem answered honestly. 'Razor shot at people. I think there is a likelihood that he will not have survived. Angela may have been taken alive to answer for her crimes.'

'But a lot of people were heading for the square,' Helena said doubtfully. 'Angry people.'

'The police were also going there,' Erimem countered. 'They may finally have fulfilled their task.'

'Maybe.' Helena didn't sound convinced.

'They have a more honest civilisation now,' Erimem said, and she held up her hand showing the time travel ring. 'I think it is time for us to return to our own time.'

'Suits me fine,' said Helena. I agreed. We all twisted our rings and I'm pretty sure we were all delighted to see that shelter disappear to be replaced a blink later by the familiar interior of Erimem's habitat.

We found Ibrahim in the kitchen making coffee. He looked up in surprise. 'You're back quick.' Then he saw the cuts and bruises we were all wearing. 'What the hell happened?' He pulled out a chair and tried to get Helena to sit.

She took the coffee from him instead. 'We're all right,' she said.

'How was the future?' Ibrahim asked.

'Disappointing,' I said.

'Very,' Erimem agreed.

Helena took a swig of the coffee and set the mug down. 'If you ever try to watch Big Brother I'm leaving you.'

You know, I think she meant it.

I don't blame her.

Later that night, lying in bed, I wondered if the future we had seen *had* to happen. We had seen it, experienced it... could we change it and stop it from happening? I've no idea how we would do that. But I was bloody sure it made me want to fight against it all the harder.

RAZOR'S LAW

NO MORE

ERIMEM

THE LAST PHARAOH

Sample chapter

Julianne Todd, Claire Bartlett and Iain McLaughlin

CHAPTER ONE

The museum was quiet.

Just the way he liked it.

Ibrahim Hadmani yanked his tie loose and felt a wonderful sense of freedom wash over him as he undid the top two buttons on his shirt. He sucked in a deep breath. Odd that it tasted so much better when he didn't have a tie up around his throat throttling him.

He glanced up at the clock high on the museum wall. A few minutes past six. The last of the visitors had been politely ushered out - at least Ibrahim hoped it had been politely - and the new term didn't start for another week. That meant most of the students who attended the university attached to the museum either hadn't arrived back in London yet or they were in the local bars and clubs getting some practice in for the alcohol and hormone fuelled carnage that would be Freshers Week.

At a few months past his thirty-sixth birthday, Ibrahim was in good shape. He went to the gym a couple of times a week and was mostly careful about what he ate. He still saw himself as a young man. He certainly ran rings around most of the younger lads at football on a Sunday morning.

But compared to the students he was a dinosaur.

He allowed himself a slight smile at the memory of his own days as a student. The current crop of kids wouldn't believe it, but whatever mayhem they indulged in, Ibrahim was pretty sure he already had the t-shirt. Been there, seen it, done it, he thought wryly.

And I enjoyed it too.

Ibrahim took a quiet stroll through the museum. Over the centuries, the London University of History and Antiquity had gained a collection of historical artefacts every bit as impressive and extraordinary as the university's reputation for scholarship and intellectual integrity. It housed items from numerous Crusades, including a cup once believed to have been the Holy Grail, and which had been the subject of a series of battles which raged over a several decades before its history was disproved. Instead, the cup was brought back to England carrying the heart of the last knight who had fallen in its defence. In another room there were relics from Agincourt. Another was devoted to Rome and its empire, which had been an interest of Ibrahim's since even before university.

Intrigued by those as he was - and as respectful of their history as any true historian would be - it was the Egyptian Collection which always captured Ibrahim. True, he was an Egyptian himself, and without the collection's presence he would not have been in London. It had been part of the deal between the Egyptian government and the university that these sacred relics of a great past would only be loaned to the museum if an Egyptian Curator was appointed, and Ibrahim had leaped at the chance when the job was offered. His family was one of the oldest in Egypt, steeped in the lore and traditions of the ancient country. As a graduate of this university himself, Ibrahim was the perfect choice to be the new curator. And more importantly for Ibrahim, it meant he could return to London for the entire ten years of the collection's loan period.

He loved the city. His schooling had all been in London, and as much as he loved Egypt, London felt like home. If he could study these amazing artefacts, while living in his favourite city, then that was a deal Ibrahim couldn't resist.

If only he didn't have to wear a damn tie.

Ibrahim pulled his tie off completely and shoved it carelessly into his pocket. After six o'clock, when the public were gone, he could dress as he saw fit. He was sure that the pharaohs whose treasures filled the room wouldn't object. He paused at a glass case and looked at the mummified remains of a young prince inside. The dry, broken skin, desiccated and aged by the passing of almost three and a half thousand years looked brittle and fragile like old paper. It was hard to believe that it had once been a young man, full of life, a man who should have ruled the world. Ibrahim said a short prayer from the Book of the Dead before moving deeper into the room.

The chamber was impossibly old. Burning torches cast flickering lights across the sandstone walls, making the hieroglyphic characters leap and jump. Each of the friezes was filled with death. Even those who couldn't read these ancient writings would have no difficulty in understanding their meaning. Bolts of lightning flew from the hand of a massive hyena-headed figure, blasting through the chests and heads of Egyptian soldiers. The detail in the carvings was incredibly intricate. The severed limbs and spraying blood of the Egyptian soldiers as they were slain by the Jackal-God's lightning was made even more disturbing by the expression of malevolent delight carved on the god's face.

In the middle of this chamber, Leon Davis was in hell.

He was in hell and he knew he was going to die.

Leon was stretched on his back across an ancient sandstone altar eight feet long by three feet wide. It stood a good four feet above the floor of the chamber. The altar was also covered with carved hieroglyphics, as violent and bloody as those on the walls. But the hieroglyphs on the altar had a different look, as if they had been filled in with a black dye. When Leon had realised what it really was inside the carvings, he had yanked and pulled at the chains. Even when he felt them slicing into his ankles and wrists he had strained every muscle in an effort to rip them free.

It was blood inside the hieroglyphs. Dried blood. And his own blood would soon be joining it unless he could somehow break free. He strained for what seemed like hours. There was no way to keep track of the time in the chamber. When his muscles ached so badly that he could barely move them, Leon yelled and screamed for help until his voice had grown hoarse and failed him. But no help had come. He hadn't expected any.

Because this couldn't be happening. Not now, not here. It just couldn't. He had even wondered if this was some kind of stunt, some English prank played at the expense of a Fresher. Maybe something more sinister? Make the Yank suffer. Show him why America shouldn't get involved in the Middle East. It was a crazy thought. Even students wouldn't go that far for a stunt. But it was no crazier than the alternative.

And he wanted to believe anything except the alternative.

Leon heard the flames on the torches crackle and the light danced. He jerked his head round. A heavy tapestry, embroidered with the same bloodlust as the hieroglyphs on the walls, had been pushed aside. The tapestry hadn't been there before. He was sure of it. But that didn't matter. He scarcely saw it. His attention was focused on the dozen figures who glided through the doorway behind the tapestry. Each wore a long, heavily embroidered robe, with a cowled hood which kept their faces in darkness.

All except for the last member of the coven.

His cloak was far more intricately decorated with scenes of mutilation and torture embroidered in the style of Egyptian paintings. Unlike the others, his cowl was pushed back, From under it, the face of a jackal stared directly at Leon. A row of sharp teeth protruded from the long snout. Blood was painted on them. No, it wasn't paint. The blood was real. Above the snout, the eyes glowed a hellish red as if lit from within.

Leon strained again. He had thought he had no strength left, but the sight of the jackal and its coven fired energy through his body and he pulled at the chains, straining with every muscle. He had run track in high school, played on the defensive line for the football team, he had wrestled. He was strong, fit. The chains had to give. They had to.

But they didn't give. The cuffs bit deeper into Leon's skin and he felt the hot flow of his own blood on his wrists. He didn't care. The blood spurred him on. He pulled harder. Felt the blood flow faster. Ignored it. Pulled. Twisted his body so that every muscle could pull at the chains. If even one came free he had a chance. A chance to fight. The chain could be a weapon. He just need to one to come loose. Just one. It had to.

It had to.

Had to…

The coven had surrounded the altar, watching Leon struggle. He felt a change in the chain. For just an instant he thought his hand come free but then it registered in his brain that the chain felt heavier. A fraction later he became aware that his limbs were heavier too. He could hardly move them. Too late, he saw the bowl of smoking incense being held close to his head by one of the coven. Smoke from the burner had drifted around Leon. It moved like a living thing, twisting its way into his nose and mouth. Even as he choked, trying to spit his sickening sweet taste of the incense from his mouth, Leon felt the paralysis spread through his body. His arms stopped moving, his legs felt dead to him and he fell back onto the altar. His breathing was shallow, painful.

He knew it was over. He just hoped that the drug would kill him before this coven could do anything worse to him. Leon's sight blurred for a moment. Instinctively, he blinked hard, trying to focus. One of the coven had pushed at one of the great sandstones in the wall and it had slid upwards allowing some sort of brightly lit computer panel to slide out of the wall in its place.

It didn't belong.

Didn't belong any more than an Egyptian sect could belong in 21st century London.

When the Jackal spoke, the voice was in English but with a slight accent. Middle East? "Have you found her?" Her? Who were they talking about? Leon was one of the first students to arrive. He had hardly seen anyone else. Except maybe that dark haired girl. What was her name? Why couldn't he remember her name? She was a Fresher, like him. English, dark haired, quite tall. One of the caretakers had called her 'posh totty'. He couldn't remember what that meant.

Now Leon couldn't remember her face. She had been pretty but what had she looked like? And what had she been wearing?

Was it this girl they were looking for?

"She is not where we expected," the Jackal's acolyte answered. He operated a few controls and pressed some buttons - did they have a laptop connected to the control panel somehow? That just seemed silly to Leon. Maybe it was a stupid dream? All of it was a dream. Lights and patterns flowed across the control panel as the acolyte seemed to track a path. "She's here," the acolyte said, pointing at part of the screen.

"Are you sure?" The jackal sounded shaken.

The acolyte nodded. "The trace leads here. I have run it three times and each time it tracks her to this location."

"So far away," the Jackal said softly. "Did her ancestors try to hide her from us? Did the coward Pharaoh think he could hide the child from Ash-Ama-Teseth? He had more knowledge than even we knew... but he could not hide her forever." The

Jackal turned and strode back to the altar. "Bring her to this place."

The acolyte bowed and operated control, his hands flicking back and forth between the control panel and the laptop. "The scans have locked to her DNA."

The Jackal nodded in satisfaction. "We must do our god honour."

Immediately he had spoken, the coven began a chant. "Imtera-ho-Seth sha lim ka veda rahoshom serium lee din sakk-daran." The chant was repeated, a low incantation uttered perfectly in unison. Everything in the ritual had to be precise, everything had to follow the instructions laid out so long before.

Years of practice and painful instruction had taught them to fear the repercussions of any failure.

One of the coven detached himself from the circle around Leon and the altar, disappearing into the shadows. He returned a moment later, carrying an ornate dagger. The blade was perhaps thirty centimetres long, and rippled like a snake sliding across the sand. The same hieroglyphs that covered the wall and altar were carved into the hilt and blade, and stained dark by the blood it had spilled over the millennia.

The Jackal took the dagger. "Our master lives in blood. Blood gives him power. Death is his life."

Two of the coven ripped Leon's shirt open, baring his chest. He couldn't move, couldn't feel any part of his body. Even his mind seemed detached.

The Jackal raised the dagger overhead. "This blade, forged by his will, bearing the blood of his enemies, the source of his exile in eternal night beyond the furthest sky, passed through the millennia, will be the instrument of his release and of his victory. It will be the instrument of this sacrifice which will bring our eternal enemy to us."

Leon saw the dagger slash downwards through the air. He was vaguely aware of a sudden pressure against his chest, but he felt no pain as the blade ripped through his skin and on, tearing deep into his heart.

"Master, take the blood of this innocent. His life is the sacrifice delivering your freedom."

Leon thought he heard the sound of some kind of electrics or machinery whining, but it was so far away and so unimportant. Was the Jackal shouting? Was he angry? It didn't matter. Leon thought briefly of his mother before everything slipped into darkness.

Ibrahim continued his stroll around the Egyptian exhibit. Somehow being here cleared his thoughts, gave them focus. He had mentally written three emails he would have to send that night. First, to the Vice Chancellor, rejecting another suggested assistant as unsuitable. Another was to Doctor Smith, who as ever, offered some intriguing suggestions, and the final one was to Carra Wilton. The email to Carra would be the most enjoyable. She was only a few years younger than Ibrahim and a spectacular flirt with a wicked sense of humour. She was also the professor who had uncovered the Tomb of the Three Princes a few years earlier. Many of the pieces in the room hailed from that find, the first time they had ever been allowed to leave Egypt.

Dozens of the large glass cases that filled the room, contained an artefact from that most recently discovered tomb in Egypt's legendary Valley of the Kings. Sarcophagi, golden death masks, canopic jars, statues and intricate works of art were all stored in the glass cases. All of the air inside the cases had either been removed to leave a vacuum or replaced with inert gases to protect the precious items from decay. After three and a half thousand years in which they had lain undisturbed by tomb robbers and untouched by weather or the wars that had raged near them, the artefacts needed protection from the minute bacteria that lived in the air, and which could attack and destroy anything organic in the collection. Pressure pads, lasers and any number of other security measures were also in place to ensure that the collection was protected from modern tomb robbers who could make tens of millions on the black market by selling the pieces to collectors.

Ibrahim stopped to look at the large frieze which had been so carefully excavated from the tomb. In the traditional ancient Egyptian style it showed three young men - obviously princes from the gold and crowns they wore, following a Pharaoh.

There was nothing unusual in that, except that the Pharaoh depicted was young and from the size in relation to the three princes, as well as the definite swell at the chest and the feminine styling of the face, the pharaoh was obviously female. Even then there was nothing actually extraordinary in that. It was unusual, certainly. The majority of pharaohs had been men but history had noted a number of female Pharaohs. Hatchepsut and Smenkhare, for instance. The odd thing about this female Pharaoh was that she was completely unknown to history. She was a mystery.

She was *his* mystery.

He had been intrigued by the tomb's discovery, sucked in by the enigma as so many people around the world had been. The difference was that unlike all of those others around the world, Ibrahim had the chance to observe the objects up close every day.

And more or less every day that's exactly what he did.

Ibrahim started the walk back to the door. He did the same circuit of the room every day. Was he becoming predictable? He checked his watch. Time to go. He was on supper duty and there would be hell to pay if Helena got home from a late shift at the hospital and he hadn't got supper ready. And picking up a pizza or fish and chips wasn't an option. Not with Helena. The downside of being in a relationship with a doctor was that she could point out the health risks in every piece of fast food Ibrahim could pick up on the way home. Of course, that wouldn't stop her tucking into whatever he bought but somewhere there would be a lecture on health. Best to save takeaways for a treat and cook something himself.

As he always did, Ibrahim stopped and stared into a glass case containing a large stone tablet. The hieroglyphs were ornate and beautifully carved - and like everyone else on the planet, Ibrahim had absolutely no idea what they said. They were an entirely separate pictographic language, similar to hieroglyphics in style but in an alphabet of characters utterly lost to the centuries. Ibrahim stared at the tablet for a few moments, willing the symbols to slide into place, to make some connection in his mind so that he could begin to understand what they said... nothing. The same as every other day.

Someone would decipher it one day. One day… And Ibrahim didn't mind that it wouldn't be him. Just sharing in the discovery would be enough.

He had taken a couple of steps towards the door when the overhead lights flickered. They dimmed for a moment then returned to their full strength. That would have to be reported to the caretakers again before he left. As with any old building, the museum's electrics were prone to occasional… eccentricities was a polite way to put it. There had been occasional flickering lights and power dips for the past few months. The electricians assured them that there was nothing to worry about. But the artefacts in the exhibit - in all of the museum's exhibits - were utterly priceless and Ibrahim wasn't ready to gamble them on the promise of an electrician who was probably overworked and underpaid. He would demand that electrics be properly investigated. If not, he could always say that he would have to recommend that the Egyptian pieces be returned to Cairo. Regretfully, of course. And, of course, the Vice Chancellor would know that Ibrahim would do nothing of the sort - but it would be enough to get the board to stump up the money for the electrics to be properly repaired.

Already beginning to compose the email to the Vice Chancellor in his head, Ibrahim headed for the door. He had taken half a dozen steps when the lights died completely, throwing the room into near total darkness. Ibrahim stopped dead still. The last thing he wanted to do was to blindly barge into one of the exhibits. He waited for his eyes to become accustomed to the dim light. As he did so, he became aware of an unusual smell. Something sharp and tangy that caught at the back of his throat. It reminded him of something. Old fairground rides. The sparks from the electric dodgems. Was that ozone?

And what the hell was producing that light that had thrown a pale blue glow around the room? What on Earth was going on? Ibrahim reached into him pocket for his mobile phone…

A flash of electricity, as brilliant as a bolt of lightning, shot across the room. Tendrils of bright blue electricity spat off in a dozen directions, arcing between the hanging light fittings and wall switches, and flashing along the fine metal borders of the display cases, dancing back and forth between any pieces of bare metal and sources of electricity. A row of lightbulbs exploded above his head and Ibrahim threw himself flat onto the floor, wrapping his arms over his head, waiting for the electricity to pass. The storm of electricity took less than fifteen second to reach its peak and then abate. To Ibrahim, it felt a lot longer. Every second he waited for the electricity to crash into his body, or the sound of one of the display cases cracking under the onslaught. He wasn't sure which would have been worse. He curled into a ball. Even when the electricity sounded like it was fading he didn't move until he was absolutely certain it had gone. Finally, Ibrahim did move, tentatively looking out into the room. A thin smoke hung in the atmosphere, there was still a strong smell of ozone and the short hairs on the back of his neck and hands were standing on end. Short bursts of residual electricity still crackled at the nearest light switch in the wall but as far as he could see none of the display cases had been damaged. It verged on a miracle and he wondered if, perhaps, some ancient Egyptian spirit had been watching over them. Naturally, he didn't believe in any of the old gods - he didn't believe in any new ones either - but he was happy to hedge his bets and offered a quick thank you to whatever deity or good fortune had protected both himself and the collection.

For the second time in a few minutes, Ibrahim reached for his mobile phone, and for the second time he was stopped. This time by a low moan from the far side of the display case he had taken refuge beside. For a fleeting moment, he had thoughts of the legends of curses and mummies but he threw them aside quickly, and hurried around the case.

A girl lay face down in the aisle between the cases. She was trying to push herself up but she couldn't seem to co-ordinate her body or her arms. She reminded him of a fawn trying to stand for the first time.

"Are you all right?" Ibrahim asked.

The girl's head swung round. She couldn't control her head either. Her eyes were glassy and unfocused, her mouth loose. She choked out a few gutteral sounds and swayed. She looked stoned. Ibrahim had seen it often enough. Which student hadn't? He thought of calling the police, but her expression changed. Her eyes focused on him for a few moments before she clamped them tightly shut in concentration. She clenched her fists until the knuckles were white and she began to control her breathing, inhaling and exhaling slowly and rhythmically.

Ibrahim guessed she was around twenty-three or twenty-four. She had the same light coffee skin-tone that he did and he guessed she was from a similar part of North Africa as himself. Her hair was long, straight and black but it was tidy, and her clothes... well, he was no expert on what girls were wearing these days but this looked like a cross between a robe and a long skirt with britches underneath. She would have been pretty, perhaps even beautiful if her face wasn't twisted in concentration.

"Are you all right?" he repeated.

The girl's dark brown eyes snapped open. "Of course I am not all right, idiot. What have you done to me? What is this place?"

"I haven't done anything to you. I just found you here. Are you hurt?"

"Of course I am hurt, fool. It feels as if a hippopotamus is trying to burst out of my head. My stomach is on fire and churning and I think I am going to..." She clutched her stomach and jack-knifed forward. She retched and threw up. It was mostly water and bile. She retched again and spat the last of the liquid from her mouth onto the floor before pulling a cloth from a pocket and wiping it across her mouth. She was still in pain but her eyes had cleared. She certainly wasn't stoned. She just looked like she had been through a hell of a shock.

Ibrahim hunkered down beside the girl. "Can I get you something? Water?"

She grimaced, looking at the pool she had just deposited on the floor. "That is probably not the wisest thing for me now." Her voice was clipped and precise. Intelligent and articulate. And definitely not a junkie, Ibrahim thought sourly. He should have known better than to make assumptions. Had she been hit by electricity or affected by it in some way?

"Do you feel well enough to stand?" Ibrahim asked.

73

The girl thought for a moment before answering. "No," she said simply. "But I cannot sit here all day." She extended a hand regally to Ibrahim. He stared at it dumbly. "You may help me stand." Her voice wasn't unkind but there was no doubt she expected Ibrahim to help her. He took her fore-arm and held gently as the girl pulled herself to her feet. She swayed woozily for a second before her balance returned. "Thank you." She smiled and the smile transformed her face. The anger and frustration had gone, quickly replaced by an intense curiosity, as she started to look around and take in her surroundings. "Where am I?" she asked.

Ibrahim answered, "The London Museum of History and Antiquities. The displays are…"

He didn't finish. The girl's voice cut across him, sharp and angry. "Why are these objects here?" she demanded, staring at the precious historical articles in the glass cases. "Why are they not in the tombs where they belong?"

The question explained a good deal. Many of his fellow Egyptians had been against sending the precious artefacts out of Egypt, especially for such a long time. The girl must have been one of the protestors. "Given how much was stolen by our own people when they raided the tombs, I think this is as safe a place as any for these beautiful objects," he said. "I make sure they are treated with respect and care."

The girl's dark brown eyes bored into Ibrahim, gauging whether he was telling the truth or not. Finally she nodded a little. "That is good," she said. "But if you are lying, I swear I will cut the tongue from your mouth and feed it to the jackals."

"What?" Ibrahim choked. She was serious. He could see it in her face. She meant every word of her threat. "Who are you?"

The girl's mouth snapped open to answer… but then she stopped. No words would come. Her mouth moved for a few seconds as she looked more and more confused. "I do not know," she answered finally.

"You don't know you own name?"

"My mind is clouded," the girl said sharply. "My memory is hidden from me."

"Really?" Maybe he had been too quick to dismiss the idea

of drugs after all.

She glared at him and Ibrahim took an involuntary step backwards. "Do not mock me, old man."

"Old?" Ibrahim was indignant. "I'm only thirty-six." It was the damned suit that made him look older.

The girl seemed to find strength in her anger, as if it focused her. "That is what I said. Old!" She swept a hand around the room and began to inspect the glass cases. "What else did you find with these objects?"

"It's a magnificent collection, isn't it?" Whether she was a student or a protestor, the girl was certainly entranced by the collection. She couldn't be all bad. "It was nearly all found in an undisturbed tomb in the Valley of the Kings. Everything in the tomb had been untouched since the tomb was sealed. It's called it the Tomb of the Three Princes and…"

"This was not in that tomb." The girl had stopped by the case containing the large stone with the mysterious pictographic writing on it.

"No," Ibrahim agreed. "That was found about twenty years ago in a cave…" He stopped. Exact details of the stone's discovery had been kept secret for fear of sending thousands of treasure hunters off into places where they would almost certainly destroy anything of historical value they might accidentally find. There had been an assumption that the stone was somehow found near or in the Tomb of the Three Princes and the Egyptian Ministry of Antiquities had simply never corrected that assumption. "How did you know it wasn't found in the tomb?"

Her eyes flickered across the stone. Almost as if she recognised it. "It was in a cave on the western ridge," she said. "It was protected by many traps."

A student certainly wouldn't have known any of that. Ibrahim doubted if anyone outside of the Ministry knew the truth about the stone's discovery. After all, three American tourists had died at the hands of the traps in the cave. If they hadn't hushed that up, it would have been a disaster for the tourist industry. "Are you from the Ministry?"

She shook her head. "No."

"Then how can you know all that?"

The girl looked at Ibrahim as if he was a very simple child unable to grasp even the simplest idea. "Because it is written on the stone."

And as she began to read, Ibrahim Hadmani's jaw dropped open.

"Only those who have passed the great desert with life intact in their bodies and whose spirit has the nobility and wisdom to survive the tests of Pharaoh will find light and darkness carved in this stone."

"You can read that?" Ibrahim breathed, utterly shocked.

The girl looked back at him with irritation. "I just did, did I not? Part of it, anyway."

"But no-one can read that," Ibrahim protested. "How can you just appear here out of nowhere and…"

The girl interrupted, reading more from the stone tablet. "Heed the warning of Mighty Pharaoh. The darkness the God-King bled to send into the far abyss shall use the power of night to rise. If it rises the land will be cast into shadow and all flesh shall wither to dust on the bone."

It wasn't possible. She couldn't be reading the tablet. Could she? "But the language on that tablet has been dead for thousands of years," Ibrahim said. "How can you read it?"

She opened her mouth to speak but again no words would come. Her delicate, pretty face creased into a frown. "I do not know."

She had to be having a joke at his expense. Playing a trick to avoid getting into trouble for being in the museum after hours. Maybe she had been the one who made the electrics go haywire. "You don't know?"

Her eyes snapped up, blazing with anger at the disbelieving tone in Ibrahim's voice. "I don't know," she repeated harshly. "I don't know…" her voice faltered, becoming uncertain. "I do not know… I do not know how I can read that. I do not know where I am. I do not know where I have come from. I do not know my name… I do not know… I do not know anything!"

Ibrahim looked at the girl. Her clothes were unusual but clean. Her eyes were confused but they had none of the tell-tale signs of alcohol or drugs. They were focused and clear and had moved intelligently, surveying the room and taking in her surroundings. She was disoriented and had definitely been in pain.

And she had read the stone… hadn't she?

Her translation fit the rhythms and speech patterns Ibrahim would have expected from that period of Egyptian history. And the repeated characters within the mysterious hieroglyphs matched her translation as best as he could tell.

And there was something else… something familiar about her. No, more than that. He wasn't sure why, but Ibrahim trusted the girl. He held out a hand. "Come with me."

"Why?" She looked at his hand suspiciously and made no attempt to take it. "Where will you take me?"

"We need to find out who you are." Ibrahim swung his arm in an arc, indicating the room around them. "And how you can read a dead language that no-one else in the world has been able to decode."

"These things are familiar to me," she said softly, pressing her forehead against the glass of a display case, as if getting closer would release her trapped memories.

"They're from the most famous tomb of recent years," Ibrahim said. "There were three royal brothers buried together. There was a fourth chamber in the tomb, which was full of great treasures but the Pharaoh who should have been there was missing. And the remarkable thing was…"

"I know this mask." The girl cut across Ibrahim's lecture. She was standing by the golden death mask. The mask which had always so intrigued Ibrahim.

"It's the mask of the Pharaoh whose tomb was empty," Ibrahim answered. "As I was saying, it's…" Ibrahim's voice tailed off. His mouth felt suddenly dry.

It was impossible.

It couldn't be.

And yet the proof was in front of him. Staring at him, dark brown eyes full of questions.

"It's you," he breathed.

The girl looked at Ibrahim in confusion and then turned back to the Death Mask.

The golden face staring blankly back at the girl was her own.

ERIMEM

THE BEAST OF STALINGRAD

Sample chapter

Ibrahim:

When the cold comes, I think of her. Her eyes were warm. Her face kind. But in the cold I remember her. I remember her and I remember Stalingrad. Sometimes I ask myself if she was real. Was anything real? The war is over now. It is eight years since it ended. Eight years since we breathed again. Eleven years since those days in Stalingrad. Was it real? Did these things happen? Does my memory lie to me? No. They happened. It was real. Erimem was real. The terrible suffering we endured… the terrible things we saw in Stalingrad… those were real also.

Andy:

It's summer in Britain. That means it's chucking down rain and there's a gale howling in off the Atlantic. If Mary Poppins tries any of her flying malarkey today she'll wind up in Norway. Jesus, it's cold. If I had balls they'd be getting frozen off. I'm actually glad I'm working in the café today. When nobody's looking I'm giving the tea urn a cuddle to get some heat in me. I might ask Ibrahim to have a word with the new Vice Chancellor about the heating. It gets switch off at the end of April every year and we don't get another sniff of it until October. This – is – Britain! Summer here has a very on-off relationship with any actual heat.

Which raises this question: having recently spent a miserable few days in the pissing rain and mud of an ancient Greek battlefield, and then realising that summer in the UK isn't the same as summer in Egypt, why did Erimem decide to go somewhere even colder? I suggested we try London in the hot summer of 1976. That way we'd get some sun on us and I could pick up classic vinyl I could flog for a fortune online. She

81

wasn't having it. She hasn't got the hang of eBay yet. She knew where she wanted to go and I wasn't shifting her mind on that.

Is she stubborn because she was a pharaoh or is it just natural? And what's my excuse? I was stupid enough to say I'd go with her. Be interesting to hear what Ibrahim's got to say about this. Or maybe not.

Ibrahim:

They're idiots and I told them as much. "Stalingrad in 1942 is just about the most dangerous place you could ever go." Andy agreed but Erimem was resolute that she was going.

It was five weeks since we'd got back from Actium. Everything considered, it had been an interesting month or so. No, that's glib. I shouldn't do that. It had been a month that mixed a lot of relief that we were alive with the guilt that Anna, who had travelled back to ancient Greece with us, had been left there after she was murdered. It was logical. There was no way we could have brought her home and had the time to save Erimem's life as well. Still, seeing her family mourning at the remembrance service hit us all hard.

I know how hard it hit me. I'm a historian. Traveling to the past, to see one of the most important moments in the history of Egypt should have been the greatest experience for me. Instead it left me asking a lot of questions, mostly about myself. I came a hell of a close to dying myself because of injuries I got on that journey. Those injuries were inflicted by people at the university I had thought of as friends.

I trust people less now.

I trust myself less.

I killed someone. The Vice Chancellor of the University. He had killed so many people and he would have been responsible for the deaths of billions. He was going to kill Erimem and Andy as well. I stopped him. A sword in the back. The logical part of my brain knows I did the right thing. I had to stop him and I did. Unfortunately, the logical part of my brain couldn't stop me remembering and it couldn't stop the nightmares. I had them almost every night. Nightmares about dying and others where I relived killing the Vice Chancellor over and over again. I don't know which was worse – the fear of my own death or realising that I was a murderer. Helena tells me it's natural, that my mind is dealing with it. She's a doctor, she should know all of this. It doesn't make me feel better, but whenever I wake from the nightmares, she's there beside me. I should shut up about her before I say something stupid and overly sentimental.

But I love that woman.

I was disappointed she wasn't as strongly against Erimem's plan as I was. But... she has always been in favour of people finding their own way in life, and since we had discovered Erimem's 'timeline' was what she called it, I think. Since we had discovered Erimem's timeline logged in the habitat's computers we had known Erimem would want to visit some of the places the computer revealed she visited at some point in her life. I just wish she hadn't chosen Stalingrad in 1942.

Andy:

I blame myself for Erimem wanting to go to Stalingrad. It was me who found that timeline of hers. Actually, the computer did all the hard work. It came up with all the places she would visit in her life, all the different times and places. It even gave names to some of them. She was interested by all of them because she could hardly remember any of them. We could tick off Actium and Alexandria. We knew she'd been there, but the others? The computer could tell us where and when she went but it didn't tell in which order or when in her own timeline it was. Were these places she had already visited in her personal past or places she still had to experience? She didn't have a clue and neither did any of the rest of us.

Erimem being Erimem, her first instinct was to pick a place and go there. She was curious about everything. It took a while to put her off the idea. We had to remind her of what had happened the last time we had all travelled through time unprepared. She didn't like it but she accepted the sense. At least I think she did.

She started at the University as a student – a student who got extra credit by acting as Ibrahim's assistant. That gave him the chance to keep an eye on her. It's really weird that she's his great great great… about a hundred and fifty-odd generations of great auntie. They seem to be okay with it anyway. Helena thinks it's hilarious. She is unbelievably cool with this whole weird set-up. I like Helena.

Erimem lives with Ibrahim and Helena now. Sort of. She lives in their airing cupboard. How Harry Potter is that? The difference is that Harry actually did live in a cupboard under the stairs – the cupboard door Erimem uses takes her into a sort of emergency escape habitat that's outside of time and space. Don't ask me. I don't know how it works. What I do know is that it's currently behind a very ordinary door and it looks like a villa from her home time with some modern stuff thrown in. I sort of designed how it looks – but whoever built the machines that control the Habitat were smart enough to know they should make it easy for idiots to work the damn thing. It was mostly just pointing the computer at information.

It felt like we'd all had a chance to stop and draw a breath after Actium. We'd been to the memorial service and somehow, we were all getting back to our normal lives. For me that included being the most hated person in my brother, Matt's life, for throwing his latest best friend out of the flat for smoking a joint. He hates me again.

Big deal.

He'd hate me worse if he wound up in the cells for a night.

I thought Erimem had settled to the idea of not visiting the places in her timeline until she rocked up to the café looking really determined about something.

"Tell me about Stalingrad," she said. "In the last century. In the time I was there."

I told her what I could. "Imagine Hell and then freeze it. A huge German army lays siege to the city in autumn and winter of 1942."

"It would be bad for the people who are there?"

"God, yeah," I agreed. "No food, no fuel. The question was whether they're starve or freeze first.

That seemed to make up her mind. "Thank you," she said and turned away. "I will need some very warm clothes."

I wanted to swear at her, but I was at work. It was quiet but there were a few of the new members of the faculty sitting having coffee. I didn't need them on my case. "You're going there, aren't you?"

She nodded. "I must." She was determined and I knew her well enough to know I'd be wasting my time trying to change her mind.

"When are you going?"

"Soon."

Honestly. What kind of crappy answer is 'soon'? If I ask my brother when he'll do the dishes, his 'soon' can mean 'never'. When a professor asks a student about an assignment 'soon' can mean 'three weeks on Wednesday'. I had no idea what Erimem's 'soon' meant. "Listen," I told her. "Tomorrow's Saturday. My brother is at some football thing until Sunday. I'll come with you."

She said no, and said I shouldn't... then she just shrugged

and agreed to it. I had no idea what was going on in her head, but whatever it was, I'd have to dig the winter clothes out of the cupboard.

Ibrahim:

I tried to talk them out of going. I told them they were a pair of idiots. Bloody fools, both of them. They weren't listening. Erimem had made up her mind that she had to go to Stalingrad and Andy was determined to go with her.

Why Stalingrad in 1942? She wouldn't answer. She just said she had to go there and she would explain later. And then she smiled and asked us to trust her. Of course I trust her. Doesn't mean I don't worry about her. I said I'd go along with them. It was a close thing for who said 'no' first, Erimem or Helena. Helena won on volume.

I'm still not used to having Egypt on the other side of a door in the flat. I know it's not really Egypt and I know it's not really a door. All the same, I'm still not used to walking through from a first floor London flat to find myself in a perfect replica of a villa overlooking the Nile. Helena seems more comfortable with it. That surprises me. I thought she would struggle to deal with all of this. Andy seems more at home with it than either of us and Erimem treats it like it's the most normal thing in the world. By today's standards I had a privileged upbringing. You know the thing. Old family, plenty of money, good schools. I came out of that with a certain confidence. It's nothing compared with upbringing she had, and even when she's not confident, she knows how to project a sense that she actually is.

The confidence she had heading to Stalingrad was genuine. If you watch her enough you can learn to read Erimem. I can also annoy her by calling her Auntie Erimem. At least she pretends to be annoyed. She was confident about this trip to Stalingrad, and she seemed to be driven. There was some purpose behind this journey. I thought about it and Helena and I talked about it in bed. We knew Erimem had gaps in her memory. Helena said it could be that those holes in her memory troubled Erimem and that perhaps making this journey to one of the places she knew she would visit would give Erimem more of a sense of control of her life. That sounded plausible enough.

"Do you think she should go?" I asked.

Helena snorted. "I think she's off her head to go." She softened her tone. "But I wouldn't dream of trying to stop her."

And that was that.

Andy:

I'd never felt cold like it. Five minutes earlier we'd been sweltering in Erimem's villa. Now, the layers of clothes didn't feel nearly warm enough. It actually hurt my face and I pulled a scarf up to cover as much of the skin on my face as it could while still letting me see. Erimem did the same.

We had arrived in a small street that cut off of a larger one. Well, I say street... is it still a street when half of it has been blown apart? The ruins of buildings were on either side. They were covered with a heavy layer of snow that smoothed the edges of the broken walls into hills. We were in the middle of a road but there were no tracks in the snow. Nothing had come through this street for a long time. There weren't even any signs of recent footprints in the snow. Of course, the snow was falling so heavily they'd have been covered in just a few hours, so maybe I was wrong. I didn't think so, though. The place had a feeling of being abandoned.

"Which way?" I asked Erimem. This was her show. She was in charge of this trip.

She looked around as much as she could. The snow was falling even heavier now. At a guess we could see fifty feet ahead of us. After she'd looked all around, she pointed along the street. "The houses seem less damaged in this direction." And she started trudging off through the snow. The way she moved, I got the feeling that she didn't have much experience with snow. Having said that, even when we had those bad winters back in, what was it? 2010 and 2011? Something like that? The snow was nothing like this. This just felt like the cold had been here forever. Walking was made even more difficult by the debris we couldn't see under the snow. The bricks and god knows what else from the wrecked houses almost did my ankles three or four times.

Maybe a hundred metres along the street it intersected another street. It looked bigger than the one we were in. Erimem had been right. The damage to this end of the street was nothing like as bad as what was behind us. The houses was all dark, though. I couldn't see lights in any of the windows. From the light – or lack of it – I guessed it was near dusk. If anyone was still living in these houses they'd surely have been some hint of light somewhere. There was nothing. I knew that a large part of the population of Stalingrad had tried to escape across the Volga. I also knew Stalin or his generals had put a stop to that. Apparently they thought their soldiers would fight harder if they knew their families were at risk. They might have been right but what a shit way to use people. But how bad must things be if they have to do something that shit to their own people? The ruins of that street behind us were a pretty good indication of how bad things were.

The street we crossed into was in better nick than the one we left but just as empty. Still too close to the Germans, I suppose. We turned left and walked on a little. A shop with nothing in the window but signs that hung at crooked angles told us we'd definitely arrived in Russia at least. The writing was definitely in Russian letters. Cyrillic, they call that alphabet, I think. No idea what they said.

We had walked maybe another hundred metres when Erimem stopped. She brushed the snow off her woolly hat and pulled it up so her ears were uncovered.

I asked, "What is it?"

She didn't need to answer. I heard them coming a few seconds later. A sort of whistling, whining sound, getting louder. I'd seen enough TV and films to know what the noise meant. "Shit. Artillery shells. Get down."

I threw myself face down into the snow, grabbing Erimem and taking her with me. We'd hardly hit the ground when one of the missiles hit a house about thirty metres away. I can't explain how loud it was. You felt the volume as much as heard it. It shook us through to our bones. Even through the snow we could feel the ground vibrating from the impact. The missiles kept coming in. We could hear them getting louder as they got closer and then the explosions. We felt the blasts from the rockets exploding. The air a weird mixture of cold and then hot before it was freezing again. It whipped and caught at our clothes as we lay there, waiting for the bombing to stop. I'm not sure how long it lasted. It felt like hours but it was probably only a minute or ninety seconds. The impacts sounded further away and then they stopped. We waited where we were, in case it started again but nothing came. You could tell it was over. Everything was quiet again except for that strange sound of large flakes of snow landing on more snow.

When we looked up the winds that whipped the blizzard had blown a lot of dust and muck away. The house that had been hit first was a ruin. The roof was almost totally gone, the walls had huge holes and bulged out like they were pregnant.

They'd collapse before long. Smoke was trailing up from inside. It was struggling to be seen in the blizzard. We struggled to our feet. The blast had left us shakier than I'd expected. We started along the street and I heard Erimem call out.

"There." She was pointing and then running as best she could on that awful ground. I need to wait for the snow to clear a bit before I could see what she was running towards. A woman was staggering away from one of the buildings near the one that had been bombed. She didn't seem to have a clue what she was doing. Her knees looked unsteady and she dropped to the snow just before Erimem got to her. I arrived not far behind Erimem who was looking at this woman with an odd mix of fascination and concern. I checked the woman's wrist. Her pulse was strong and steady.

"She's definitely alive," I said. "But she won't be if she lies about out here much longer."

We examined her as much as we could. She was maybe twenty or twenty two. She could have been younger or older, it was hard to tell. She looked more dead than alive but that was down to the way hunger had make her face too thin and lack of proper nutrition had left her skin grey. At least there didn't seem to be any fresh cuts or scrapes on her. "I think she was probably caught by a bit of the shockwave," I told Erimem. "She's been lucky."

Erimem nodded, looking around. "We must get her out of this snow before she freezes."

The woman's eyelids moved and she moaned. "She's coming around."

Her eyes opened and she tried to focus on us for a second.

And then she started screaming.

ERIMEM

THE LAST PHARAOH
A novel by Iain McLaughlin and Claire Bartlett

THE BEAST OF STALINGRAD
A novella by Iain McLaughlin

INTO THE UNKNOWN
an Anthology including stories by Jim Mortimore

PRIME IMPERATIVE
A novella by Julianne Todd

A PHARAOH OF MARS
A novel by Jim Mortimore

BUCCANEER
A novella by Iain McLaughlin

Available soon from
THEBES PUBLISHING

1001 COMPLETELY RANDOM DOCTOR WHO FACTS

by Claire Bartlett

Do you know when 12th Doctor Peter Capaldi was originally invited to test for the role?

Do you know who designed the Cybermen?
Or which professional teams Matt Smith played football for?
Or what links H Rider Haggard with the Third Doctor?
Or which villainous henchman was actually an opera singer?

This book is packed with 1001 facts about DOCTOR WHO, the world's longest running science fiction programme. As well as covering the TV show, there are facts about the Doctor's adventures in print, on audio, at the cinema and in the theatre. Even the most hardened fan will find there are some facts in here they didn't know about DOCTOR WHO.

Available soon from
THEBES PUBLISHING

THE ULTIMATE DOCTOR WHO FAN QUIZ BOOK

by Christopher Samuel Stone

How well do you know Doctor Who?

This book has questions of varying difficulty to test the knowledge of new fans and long-time aficionados of the world's favourite time traveller.

The book covers more than fifty years of adventures on TV and also his exploits on film, on stage, on audio and in novels. The ultimate challenge for a Doctor Who fan.

ERIMEM